good deed rain

47 Books by Allen Frost

...Ohio Trio...Bowl of Water...
...Another Life...Home Recordings...
...The Mermaid Translation...The Selected
Correspondence of Kenneth Patchen...
...The Wonderful Stupid Man...
...Saint Lemonade...Playground...Roosevelt...
...5 Novels...The Sylvan Moore Show...
...Town in a Cloud...A Flutter of Birds
Passing Through Heaven: A Tribute to Robert
Sund.......At the Edge of America.......
....Lake Erie Submarine....The Book of Ticks....
.........I Can Only Imagine.........
...The Orphanage of Abandoned Teenagers...
...Different Planet...Go With the Flow: A
Tribute to Clyde Sanborn...Homeless Sutra...
..The Lake Walker..A Hundred Dreams Ago..
....Almost Animals....The Robotic Age....
....Kennedy....Fable....Elbows & Knees:
Essays and Plays....The Last Paper Stars....
...Walt Amherst is Awake...When You Smile
You Let in Light....Pinocchio in America....
....Florida....Blue Anthem Wailing....
...The Welfare Office...Island Air...
...Imaginary Someone...Violet of the Silent
Movies....The Tin Can Telephone....
....Heaven Crayon....Old Salt....
...A Field of Cabbages...River Road...
....The Puttering Marvel....
...Something Bright...
..The Trillium Witch..

The
TRILLIUM
WITCH

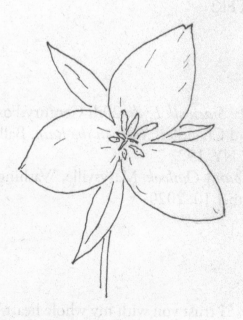

The TRILLIUM WITCH © 2021
Allen Frost, Good Deed Rain
Bellingham, Washington
ISBN 978-1-63901-614-3

Writing & Drawings: Allen Frost
Cover Photograph: Rosa Frost
Cover Production: Katrina Svoboda
Thanks to Larry Smith for reading
Apple: TFK!

Credits:
Where the Sidewalk Ends, 20th Century Fox, 1950.
Raymond Chandler, *Killer in the Rain*, Ballantine
  Books, NY, 1972.
North County Outlook, Marysville, Washington,
  November 10, 2020.

"I trust you with my whole heart."
—*Where the Sidewalk Ends*

The TRILLIUM WITCH

Allen Frost

Good Deed Rain ◊ Bellingham, Washington ◊ 2021

"Not being bullet-proof is an idea I've had to get used to."

—Raymond Chandler

The catwalk has suffered corrosion over the years and is no longer safe to walk on.

—*North County Outlook*

the CHAPTERS

CHAPTER 1
UMBRELLAS

Howard Plaid pressed the intercom button and lied, "Hello, this is Harvey Stewart, the umbrella salesman."

Suddenly the iron gate in front of his car began to roll open. It was true he had a briefcase full of umbrellas on the backseat, but he was no salesman. Howard Plaid was a detective. As he drove past the gateposts, Howard rolled up the car window.

He was surprised he was in so easily. Trillium was the name of their town. It was spelled out on movie theaters, laundromats, pizza boxes, newspapers, on water towers and the sides of garbage trucks. And now Howard was on his way to meet the Great and Powerful Oz. He might have been intimidated, but he didn't show it. He kept his eyes on the paved road as it turned into woods.

There were stories about the Trillium estate. People said there were tigers roaming the grounds. Like the rest of town, Howard half-believed the rumors.

The car rattled between cedar trees big as pillars. He gripped the wheel. If there were tigers, they could be anywhere and one slice of a paw would tear his cardboard car in half. Then what would he do—fend off tigers with an umbrella? Be glad it didn't come to that. The driveway broke free of the shadows and he steered into an open lawn the size of Wrigley Field.

Plaid was expecting a mansion out there in the middle. The Trilliums were millionaires—the town was named after them—wouldn't there be something like the Lincoln Memorial? Instead, the driveway led to a simple looking two-story house. It was light blue with white trimmed windows, steps that led to a porch. On top of the chimney was a twig-like TV antenna. It was a pleasant looking old-fashioned house. It would have been at home in a 20th century city neighborhood with kids drawing chalk pictures on the sidewalk in front, all the sounds of the block making ocean around it. Out here all alone it was only one note of a piano.

The paving ended, the car wheels rolled over mowed grass. The umbrellas rattled in the backseat. How did he know the Trilliums were in the market for umbrellas? He had his suspicions. The police department told him to find out if they were true. It was Howard Plaid's idea that only an umbrella salesman could get this close. So far, so good.

Otto Trillium was waiting behind the screen door. He patiently watched the little car approach and stop, and he saw the man who called himself Harvey Stewart get out and reach behind the seat for a bundle of umbrellas. Otto chuckled at the sight of the unwieldy bouquet. He wondered how long he would be able to play along.

Howard knew there was a chance he was being watched. It was a sixth sense. That was a detective's sense, a prickling, when you knew you were under surveillance. He picked up the Hurricane 100 and another couple models and stuffed them under his arm. Then he kicked the car door closed.

The house looked like one of those castles plunked in an aquarium tank at the pet store. Sometimes some bubbles would climb out the chimneys. The goldfish didn't care, they were used to it. A blue house sitting beneath a gray sky. A patch of bright sunlight crept across the wide lawn.

Howard's sixth sense also told him he was walking into trouble, but he didn't listen. There was always a chance of trouble, being alive meant taking chances all the time. It wasn't easy being a detective, nothing like the movies. He had bills that kept reappearing in the mailbox. Maybe it was a wild goose chase, but he was still hoping he would find what he was sent here for. He saw the crooked shape of the old man in the driveway and waved. He hoped this ruse would work, he didn't know a lot about umbrellas, all he needed was information.

Otto Trillium waved back, and in another moment

when the salesman got closer, he called, "Are you Harvey Stewart?" He just wanted to hear the answer.

Howard stopped at the stairs and thought for a second and said, "At this moment in time, I am."

That answer was good enough for Otto to open the door to let him in.

"Say, this is quite a place you've got here, Mr. Trillium. I have to admit, I was expecting one of those *Gone With the Wind* setups. This is real downhome."

"This is the house I grew up in," Trillium said. "I had it moved here all the way across country."

Howard smiled. "You're a sentimentalist."

"There isn't anything I wouldn't do for my family."

"Yes, I can tell," Howard let his umbrellas clatter about his feet. He quickly eyed the room—the fireplace, the pictures on the mantlepiece, the couch, the low table in front of it covered with books and magazines and to his right the stairs that walked up to the second floor. He was looking for clues the daughter might have left behind. "So...Is it just you living here?"

Otto Trillium said, "At this moment in time."

That answer was just as tactful as Howard's. He let it ride and went on with his pitch. "Then I suppose one umbrella will do." He bent and gathered the collection, quick to respond, "I've brought along many fine examples. For instance, if you're faced with

a light rain, this is your savior. Notice the action..."
He flicked the button and a black circle sprung into
view. "Look at that!" He seemed to have surprised
himself—it was like holding an owl that suddenly
spread its wings. He held it above his head and gave it
a spin. If any rain was falling from the ceiling, he was
fully prepared.

"That's very impressive," Otto said.

"Of course, I have umbrellas for all kinds of weather
conditions, but to be truly protected from the rain, so
that not a single drop of water could reach you, there's
nothing like Aqua Bodyguard. All you need to do is
press the activator and you're surrounded in a sealed,
impenetrable cocoon. Why, with this one you could
fall in the sea and—"

"You sure know your umbrellas, Mr. Stewart," said
Otto.

"Well, sure, it's my business to—"

"Or should I say, *Mr. Plaid?*"

In that startled moment, Howard nearly activated
the Aqua Bodyguard—one accidental twitch and he
could have been standing inside a rubber bubble. He
could have made his exit that way, blundering for the
door, rolling over the lawn back to his car. He stole a
breath from the quiet room.

Otto smiled. "Since my daughter disappeared, I've
heard the promises of charlatans and fakes. I was able

to fend off those intruders and masqueraders. It was you I was waiting for, Mr. Plaid, and I'm not surprised you're here. I've been expecting a visit from the police department. The fact that they went out of their way to hire a detective disguised as an umbrella salesman shows at least a little ingenuity on your part. You're looking for my daughter, aren't you?"

Howard let his breath out. None of his umbrellas had done their jobs, he had been spotted right through, "That's true."

"Then allow me to make a confession—I am too. I haven't seen her since the police began their sweep of the city." Otto Trillium collapsed in the chair next to the fireplace and pressed a hand over his eyes. "I have to be sure that she is safe, Mr. Plaid. That's a parent's job. I know you know that's true, Mr. Plaid. I know you've been in the same dilemma as I. Ten years ago it was your daughter, now it's mine."

Howard stood there holding umbrellas and he remembered. Police holding buckets surrounding the wet clothes left on the pavement.

"Have a seat, Mr. Plaid. You look like you're ready to fall."

Howard sighed into the other armchair by the fire.

"I know you have another job, the reason you're here is for the police. But I'm sure you can sympathize with my situation. I need your help finding her before the police do. Who would you rather work for? What job do you think is really more important? What does your heart tell you?"

Howard didn't have to ask his heart, only a ruin was left there. One of those crumbles you might see in Rome or something left on the cliffs above the Irish Sea. Ten years was a long time to feel that way.

"At least find her for me, please. Let me know where she is before you tell the police."

Howard was silent. He was thinking. One good thing about this turn of events...he wouldn't have to try and sell any umbrellas.

CHAPTER 2

WITCHES in the CELLAR

Howard Plaid drove back into the gloom, deep as night, that feasted among the thick cover of the trees. He steered with a paper bag on his lap ready at a moment's notice to toss it out the open window. It was a parting gift from his new client.

"Oh—" Otto Trillium had caught Howard before he left for his cardboard car. "You've heard rumors of wildlife on my land?"

Howard paused in the doorway with his umbrellas.

"Wait here a second," Trillium told him. He hurried from the room. Howard saw him go through another room into kitchen light at the end of the house. He heard the sound of a refrigerator open and close. A silverware drawer shucked open, paper rustled. Howard could see a garden out the distant kitchen window, a few sunflowers tall enough to peer over the sill.

When Trillium reappeared, he was carrying a brown paper bag. He crossed the moss green carpet and held it out to his guest. "If you get chased by any tigers, just throw this to them."

That's why Howard drove with the window rolled down, flooding himself with the cool wind and the earthy shadows. His eyes darted to either side of the narrow road. The engine whined. The little house in the middle of the meadow disappeared from the rearview mirror. The accelerator pedal was floored, but how fast could a cardboard car go?

The steering wheel shuddered as he took the last corner and saw the gate ahead. He had to slow down but that was okay, there weren't any tigers chasing him, and as he approached it, the iron gate began to creak open. Sunshine made long shadows of the bars.

He reached blindly over the dashboard and opened the glove compartment and got a crumpled cigarette pack. Smoking in a paper car might seem dangerous but he was careful lighting up and pushing his lighter back into his coat pocket. Beside him was a tin can getting full of crushed cigarettes. He wouldn't think of dropping one on the floor.

The car slipped out the gate and he breathed out smoke. A few clouds were formed over the bay and they drifted closer. Summer was over, they were carrying the first rain of autumn and winter. It wouldn't be much, not yet, the clouds had to remember how to rain, but it would be enough to make the streets shine in an hour. He would be home by then—everything stopped in the rain—he couldn't drive in it; his car would melt.

He stubbed out his cigarette against the inside of

the can and put it in his coat pocket for later. That's all he needed for now, he was trying to quit.

"I'll look for her," was what Howard told Trillium before he left. "When I find her, you'll be the first to know."

The car shook. The city was in sight. He saw the Leopold building and the tower of the Avalon Theatre. The red neon letters on the *Herald* roof were already glowing. Plaid was letting the car drive itself. He had been a detective long enough to know that sometimes the unseen and unforeseen had a hand in unraveling the mystery. You needed that help. Especially when you were looking for a witch.

He caught a break on Lincoln Street. He slowed and parked across from a fire engine. The hose ran from it into the basement window of a gray one-story house. A small crowd had formed at the back of the truck, three firemen and a fat man wearing a white t-shirt. They all stared at the house while they talked and as Howard neared on the sidewalk, he overhead them.

A fireman was saying it wasn't unusual to find a witch in a cellar, "When it looks like rain is on the way, they look for somewhere to hide."

"Two witches!" the man in the t-shirt said. It was his house. When he found the witches, he locked the cellar door and called the fire department immediately just like you're supposed to do. He was excited. He waved a cigar then screwed it to his mouth. Water was turning his basement into a pond. He sweated and clapped his hands. "There's two witches in there!"

That's all Howard needed to know. This was that sign he was hoping for. He edged away from the truck and followed the sidewalk back to the driveway where a tall thick hedge grew. Howard slipped behind it, let it hide him from view and he hurried along its wall to the backyard. Squeezing through a gap between branches, he found himself in the grassy lot behind the fat man's house. But Howard wasn't alone. Staked to a chain in middle was a barking dog. It wasn't a tiger, wasn't nearly as ferocious, but Howard reached in his coat pocket, pawed around the Rain Tamer pellets and removed the paper bag Trillium gave him. "Here you go!" he said and lobbed it. The barking stopped as the dog pounced on the bag full of meat, shredding the paper, turning into a shark.

Howard quickly moved across the patchy grass towards the house. This is the sort of world a detective finds themselves in. They have long since adapted to the dangers. The waxy leaves of the tree next door blinked with the fire truck's red lights. Howard was lucky, the kitchen door was unlocked.

He entered and gave the room a quick onceover. A pot of stew burned on the stovetop. A plaid window curtain cut off the view outside. A chair sat waiting at a little table set with a white empty bowl and a spoon and the day's *Herald*. The big fellow in the t-shirt must have been looking forward to that stew before he heard something downstairs. Another chair was propped against the door leading to the cellar. Now the only noise down there was the steady rush of water flooding in. The house sounded like a torpedoed ship.

Howard turned off the burner on his way to the door. He removed the chair barricade and turned the latch with a bone-like click. He twisted his shoulder to the door, braced in case a pair of witches might shoot out.

Down a steep narrow staircase, the water swirled and foamed. It was already deep and getting deeper by the moment. "Hello?" He took a step. The fat man had left the lights on in the cellar, he must have been in a terrible panic to get to the phone. "Does anyone need help?" he called.

Three steps past the light switch more of the cellar came into view.

Boxes floated like flotsam. A shoe. The jet stream from the firehose churned in one corner and across from it, pressed to the wall on top of a table cluttered with tools, two witches glared back at him. They didn't have long before the water would splash over their black leather shoes. They didn't have long before that

27

driving current would melt them away. They stared at Howard in helpless fear. They were witches, but they were only girls.

Howard shouted over the roar, "I'm here to help! There isn't much time!" He counted it lucky that he had been peddling umbrellas today—or maybe it wasn't luck—it was probably all part of the plan. He stuck a hand in his pocket and clawed out the few Rain Tamers he had. "I'm going to throw you these pellets. All you need to do is hold one tight and break the seal. It will form a waterproof layer around you and you can walk out of here." That was enough talk, he had to act fast. He descended to the edge of the rising tide. "Ready?"

They stared with their hands outstretched and he tossed what he had.

"Good catch!" he grinned. The water was breaking over their table, stopped only by the cut pine planks of a birdhouse in progress. "Now hurry! Each of you take one and tear the band!"

They did as he said and suddenly, just like magic, they became waterproof. The worktable creaked under the appearance of two rubber encased witches.

Howard took another step into the cold water. He held out a hand, "This way! Let's get you out of here, follow me!" The water was over his knees as he reached out. "Don't worry, I'll get you out of here."

Pushing a floating empty cooler out of his way, Howard grasped the mitten-like hand of the first girl and pulled. They came along quickly, connected to each other like a pair of galoshes, splashing, finding the stairs and thudding up after him.

He didn't know if the kitchen would be crowded with witchfinders, but the door popped open and it was just as it was before.

A still-life of stew caught like a cobweb in the air. On the wallpaper was a cheap plastic clock. Only two minutes had gone by. Howard rushed them, their feet like ducks on the linoleum, on to the next door, outside.

The sun was hidden behind a cloud. The dog was conked out in the middle of the yard. It ate all that tiger meat, even the paper bag. There was a strong possibility that Trillium gave him a sleeping potion for tigers. Howard didn't have time to worry about the dog, it would have to lie there until it got discovered.

Two balloon shapes trailed him nervously, scuffing across the lawn. He could feel the faint premonition of rain on his skin, enough to make a witch curl her toes.

They stopped behind a cedar fence on the edge of a neighbor's property. "Do you have somewhere safe you can go?" He held out his palm, "It's going to start raining pretty soon."

"We have other places," came a muffled reply. "Thank you."

Before they left, before they floated like dirigibles down the street, Howard asked, "Do you know Dorothy Trillium? I need to find her."

There were eyes, round plastic patches riveted onto the Rain Tamer suits that stared back at him like owls.

CHAPTER 3
MYSTERY SOUP

Howard Plaid lived in a detached garage in an alley off Myrtle Street. His home was the apartment above a parked car. It was a good place, quiet, only disturbed by the few cars that used the dirt alley, and birds sang in the big chestnut tree next door. A few cats wandered about. He wasn't at home much anyway, his work took up most of his day.

The rain didn't amount to much. Any witches out there shouldn't have any trouble staying dry.

He stared at the stove and the thought must have crossed his mind: the pot on the burner and the can next to it resembled the scene in the fat man's kitchen. Then again, it couldn't have been too uncommon a scene around town at this time. The daylight was fading, it was an easy meal to make. Also, it wasn't stew. The plain white can was labeled Mystery Soup. There could have been just about anything in it, possibly even stew…If that were true, then Howard would surely be reminded of that kitchen on Lincoln Street.

He opened the silverware drawer and got a can opener and went to work on the round tin lid. Hidden below that silver circle, the Mystery Soup was green as a pond. He hoped it was spinach and nettles, but as he poured it into the pan he was in for a surprise. There was a reason it was called Mystery Soup. Tangled in what looked like weeds, a turtle kicked its feet. Who would have guessed it was turtle soup? It paddled to the steep edge of the pan, bumping its head, looking for a way out.

"Hold on," Howard told it. This was his day for saving lives. He used a ladle to scoop it onto his hand. Its legs rocked back and forth. "I'll take you outside," he decided. He didn't bother with a coat, as he slipped his feet back into his shoes and opened the door.

Night was just around the corner. The wooden stairs were still wet from the rain, slippery, so he took them carefully. It wouldn't do for a detective to die holding a lime-sized turtle.

Someone's radio played a couple houses away. A crow called from the chestnut tree. The gutter beside him dripped. The air had that clean fresh smell washed by water as if the whole town had been run through a laundromat. He held the turtle shell between his thumb and forefinger like a skipping stone. It could bounce down the puddles in the alley if he tried. A good throw could take it all the way to the park. Luckily for the turtle, Howard had no such intention. He turned at the bottom of the stairs and took the path around the garage to the garden.

There wasn't much of a garden now, the summer flowers had dried to brown, leaving brittle stalks beside the fence. Still, a turtle would find it a better place to be than a tin can. The chestnut tree had thrown a heavy shadow over the garden and Howard stepped carefully off the path, over the Martian aqueduct. Some people had model train sets, his wife had made an elaborate scale replica of the canals on the Elysium Plains. It crawled across the garden on pillared legs, carrying a trickle of rain. Miranda and their daughter used to spend hours out here...Howard's wife even tried to grow Martian flowers but not one of them could survive. She never stopped trying though. She ordered seed packets sent by rocket.

"You'll like it here," Howard told the turtle. He bent down beside a pool not much bigger than a queen-size bed. Leaves floated on it like handprints on glass. He set the turtle on a mossy stone. After all that time in a soup can it needed a little time to get used to the world. Not that long though.

As Howard stood back up, the turtle dropped off into the pond and was gone. The water was too dark to tell where it went and the sky was too. He heard the crow again. About this time every night they would follow each other in twos and threes and go in packs over the roofs and trees headed for their roost in the park. He counted five flying by. Then he said,

"Good dreams, turtle," and left the garden.

Something clattered at the top of the stairs and took to the air, something black, bigger than a crow, blotted against the nickel sky. It vanished before he could tell if it was a bird or a witch. He had seen witches before, gliding across the face of the moon. Joining in with the geese formation flying south. At one time their daughter used to ride a broom back and forth across the yard.

But the city was on the offense to get rid of them. The fire department, the police, every witch dowser and cheap detective they could raise. That's how Howard Plaid was drawn into it.

A few more leaves tumbled off the old chestnut tree. They floated clumsily overhead.

Howard didn't seem too concerned as he took to the stairs. If a witch had been by, it wasn't the first one at this house.

At the top of the stairway there were signs something had been and gone. The dish he left for the alley cats was empty and pushed aside from where it had been. And there was a yellow card tipped into the crack of the door frame. He removed the card and read it:

NOTICE !

Water service will be interrupted

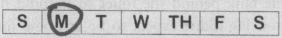

S	(M)	T	W	TH	F	S

from **7:30 am** to **6:00 pm**

on **11·9·2020**

for repairs to system

DEPARTMENT OF PUBLIC WORKS
PHONE (360) 778.7700

M:\PW\Data\Administration\Operations\Admin\Master Forms\Water

They were turning the water off tomorrow. It must be the construction on Myrtle Street. They had been digging up the sidewalk for weeks. 7:30 was pretty early. Howard liked to start the day with coffee. He opened the door slowly, thinking about a long day without water. At least the Department of Public Works gave him a little time to prepare. Time enough to fill the bathtub and every pot, pan and cup in the kitchen. He would make his house an oasis. If Bedouins with a train of camels appeared in the driveway tomorrow afternoon, Howard would be prepared to make them welcome.

He started with the bathroom, running cold water in the tub. It wasn't like he needed that much, enough to refill the tank behind the toilet so it could flush a few times. He didn't expect to be at home much anyway, after breakfast he would be out looking for the next witch clue. With the racket of Niagara Falls behind him, Howard opened the mirrored cabinet above the sink. He kept his toothbrush on a narrow shelf, a tube of Colgate, a bottle of aspirin and a water pistol.

Maybe that was why he opened that mirrored door, to get that gun. He stared at it hard, the way someone watches for an echo to come back from a long way away.

"You're not keeping that gun in our house," Miranda was telling him. "What if our daughter finds it?" He saw the look on her face as her voice dropped to a whisper, "Howard, it could kill her."

After waiting a hollow moment, he was reaching for the plastic gun when his hand froze. The telephone in the other room was ringing.

Anytime the phone rang, it was Miranda he saw at the other end of miles. She told him she would get in touch one day, when she could. Until then he was tied up in telephone wire and every time he heard the ring, he thought of her.

He shut the cabinet, turned off the gushing bathtub and went quickly into the next room. Maybe it was her this time. He grabbed the receiver and said, "Hello?" He listened to a background noise, steady and loud as a train station, a loud crowd, a brass band grinding gears, and then a woman's voice said his name.

CHAPTER 4
The TRILLIUM WITCH

Dorothy Trillium hung up the payphone. Two sets of legs in a horse costume trotted past her. Another busy showtime at the Avalon. She pushed the feathers out of her face as some dancing girls brushed by, called by the music and the spot warm as sunlight on the stage.

She pressed the coin return and got her quarter back. She knew who Howard Plaid was. She had seen him in her crystal ball, and she knew he was looking for her. She knew her father was worried about her being out in the dangerous world and the crystal ball showed him when he hired Plaid. It was plain as day. Well aware of all of this, why would she call Howard Plaid? Obviously, she thanked him for saving the two witches, but there was something more, something she caught from a crystal ball movie long before. She felt something rare.

Ahead of her and down the hall just before the Exit door on the far wall, she opened the door marked with a crooked tinfoil star.

The Great Marconi was waiting for her. After their performance every night, they met in his dressing room to go over details: what went right and what needed work in their act. Since she became his new partner a month ago, little went wrong.

Marconi already had a cup of instant coffee steaming at her side of the folding card table. He held his cup in a shaky hand. "Aha!" he grinned as she entered the small, crowded room. "Hello Dorothy!" The jar of coffee crystals rocked on the wobbling table while he staggered to stand on his wooden leg.

She motioned him to sit back down, reached and caught the jar and settled it. She saw a brief look of pain on the magician's face as he dropped to the hard chair. The pegleg he wore connected him to the shadows under the table again.

He recovered and beamed, "That was quite a show! Did you hear that applause? I could have sworn you were flying! I didn't even see the guidewires." He took a quick sip of coffee while she sat across from him. "You know, every day I count my lucky stars—what a stroke of good fortune you came into my life."

"Mr. Marconi—"

"Really and truly, there are times I believe your magic is real. I can't ever begin to thank you enough. For the first time in years this act is—"

"Mr. Marconi," she insisted, "I have to tell you something: I'm just as thankful for all you've done for me; it's been quite an experience working with you." Her eyes darted to the torn poster taped to the wall.

The Great Marconi commanding a tea set to float in the air. She took a breath. "Which is why it's so difficult to tell you that it's time for me to leave."

He didn't say anything for a moment. But she knew she had stung an old man used to pain. He tried to hide it like a card shoved up his worn tuxedo sleeve.

"Mr. Marconi…" she held a hand across the table, "I—"

"You never touch your coffee," he said in a voice that cracked. "It never occurred to me that you didn't like it."

"Oh, Mr. Marconi." She squeezed his dry hand. She couldn't cry—the tears would have burned her face.

He patted her hand. "No, it's okay my dear, I understand. To be honest, you deserve your own magic show." He tried to laugh. "You'd run me right off the stage though!"

"I'd never do that, Mr. Marconi. I'm done with show business, I'd like something a little more out of the limelight."

"Like accounting?"

"Sure," she smiled. "Something like that."

"You have another job lined up?"

"Don't worry about me, Mr. Marconi. I'll be alright."

He nodded. "I know you will. Whatever you do."

"I'll stop by the place and get my suitcase." She stood.

"You really are leaving." It dawned on him.

"I really am." And she was. She took her black coat off the hook on the door and put it over her red costume dress. She tugged off her long blonde wig and stuffed it in her bag. Out on the street no one would think she was the girl who flew in the Avalon. She reached for the door. Saying goodbye was coming more and more often and she didn't like it. That seemed to be the world she was in. The door opened, shut, and she was gone before The Great Marconi could move from his chair.

At first, he didn't realize. He stood beside the table staring at the door. Then when he took a step towards where Dorothy had been, and another step, he discovered what she had done. "The only real magic," he told her when she first asked for a job with him, "is believing in magic." He believed. He looked at the floor. The pegleg wasn't there. He had two legs, two feet in matching scuffed wingtip shoes. He opened his mouth and took a bite of the air.

A family of tap dancers clattered down the hall towards the stage, and around them and out the Exit door into the alley went Dorothy. She was hidden under the hood of her coat with her hands tucked into the deep pockets. It was night, the streetlights sparked

46

on the parked wet cars. It wasn't raining but a witch couldn't take chances with the weather. Her coat was like an anchovy tin with her crawled in.

Franklin Avenue was a harbor at night, with the lights of ships coming and going. On the corner, she went across to the next block. She wasn't far from Marconi's loft above the Eastlake Café.

She glanced back over her shoulder to make sure Marconi wasn't running after her. The coast was clear. She smiled picturing that old magician with his new leg, dancing like Fred Astaire.

The café spread light carpets on the sidewalk. The windows hummed with the music inside. For a month, Dorothy started her morning there. Not anymore. She was moving across town, her bag was already packed upstairs.

Around the other side of the café, a service alley made a narrow channel. Dumpsters, garbage cans, slumping wires overhead and a metal balcony covered with flowerpots. She stopped under it and said, "Broom." She knew the alley would be empty, nobody would see, this would save her from going up into that room again.

The balcony door pushed open and her broom appeared. It floated over the railing carrying her suitcase. Dorothy held out her hands as it descended, meandering in a spiral like a maple leaf...it wasn't in any rush. The broom liked living in The Great Marconi's apartment, it would miss it. The dust lay like polish on trophies and framed photographs. The old wooden floors creaked when you swept.

She caught the broom by the handle, held it horizontal so the suitcase rocked from its grip.

Time to say goodbye to the room upstairs, time to say goodbye to the Eastlake Café. Its narrow kitchen window was blurred from years of steam. The dishwashing machine was running, washing a load of glassware that rattled and chimed like bells. She would miss the smell of breakfast.

Her eyes said goodbye, another one on top of so many. She tugged the hood tighter around her face and got on her broom and instantly got lost in the breeze, straight up.

Over on Myrtle Street, not far as the crow flies, Howard Plaid was asleep. A long day drove him to that. The water he poured in the bathtub was slowly letting itself down the drain, past the rubber stopper. It never was a perfect fit.

Other witches were out in the dark, Dorothy could feel their presence like radar. One was down below. Down on Cornwall Avenue.

Dorothy kicked her feet, enough for the broom to drop that way. She saw a girl sweeping the sidewalk as if doing some nameless good deed. So much passed by unseen in the city but Dorothy landed next to her. "Are you okay?"

A girl, younger than her, stopped sweeping and held her broom hopelessly. "It doesn't work! I can't fly!"

Dorothy put a hand on the girl's shoulder and calmed her.

A couple walked past them. Dorothy heard them mutter, "Sweeping... Why are they doing that at night?" That was good, it meant they didn't know what was really happening.

The passing cars lit them. A green traffic light shined on Dorothy. Cornwall Ave was busy with night people. The two witches fit right in. Dorothy set down her broom and suitcase and was telling the girl something lost to the sound of the road and another café playing music not far away. A bus went by. A loud rush of yellow windows and dull chrome. When it passed, there were no witches on the sidewalk.

Dorothy could have flown in the direction of her new home but instead she turned a hundred feet above Holly on the way to Myrtle Street. She skimmed the top of a chestnut tree.

Howard Plaid was sleeping. Nothing was happening in his dream. He lay under crumpled blankets like a dead man. The ashtray next to him smoldered. He had an alarm clock, but he forgot

49

to wind it. It was quiet as a turtle on the bedside table.

Dorothy landed on the garage roof and crept silently to where it hung over his window. She set her suitcase and broom down and lay beside them, to look over the gutter.

If Howard had been awake, he would have seen the shadow moving across his wall. It was the same kind he saw after his daughter died—it was the shadow of a witch. Soft as a bee, it landed on his pillow. Up on the roof, Dorothy could see into his dream. The shadow hovered its hand above Howard, an inch from his eyes, and gave him a different dream.

All of a sudden he was in a field…it felt familiar. For a second he remembered the Trillium house in the middle of the forest. But this was a field at night. The moon looked big as a Chinese gong. Candles were lit in the windows of the two-story house in the field. He was already walking towards it; he couldn't help it. The walls were made of chocolate, candy bars grew from the flowerboxes, and when he pressed the jellybean doorbell, he was let in.

CHAPTER 5
ASH & FILTERS

Dorothy Trillium awoke to ravens. Their beaks and claws tapped and scratched overhead, their clucks and voices cracked like ripping tin.

The water tower shined above the trees. A pair of ravens took off from it, done with their alarm clock job. Morning was blue and gold and all the birds below were singing like mad.

Soon, a hatch cover twisted open and Dorothy looked out. This tall water tower was the last place you would expect a witch. She happened to know it was empty though. None of the town's water towers were full. The Trillium Corporation kept them that way. Otto was a businessman who lived by the rules of supply and demand and scarcity was his religion. A dry hot summer was over, some long months of rain were coming. Water would be recaptured, stored, and metered out for a price. Trillium was behind every drop from every faucet, the town counted on that. Water was life…for everyone but a witch.

Dorothy moved from the sunlight, grabbed the hatch cover and shut it. Nobody had seen her, nobody thought to look up at the rusted plating. The faded painted words on it, TRILLIUM, could have spelled

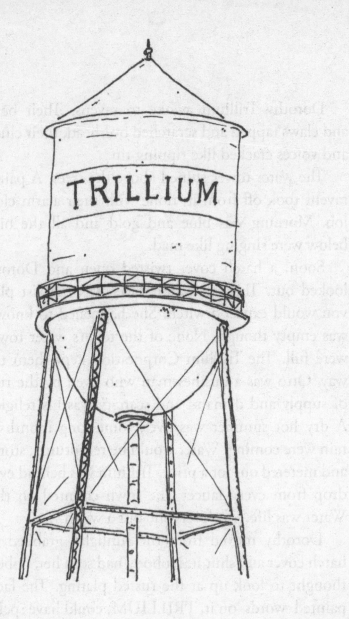

CHICAGO. It didn't matter, nobody read it. The 120 foot tower was just another ordinary part of the neighborhood.

The birds kept on singing in the bonsai forest crowded below. It was a good place to see chickadees, towhees, thrush and warblers and sparrows. That's what brought birdwatchers to this spot. There were three of them in the brush, a little family, with binoculars for eyes.

Their son was the only one not looking for birds. He was counting rusted bolts on the catwalk. "A hundred forty two...a hundred forty three..." His parents were looking for a cedar waxwing—they just heard its unique squeak, it had to be nearby. At the sound of "a hundred forty nine," the hatch opened again. For only a second, the boy saw a blur in the air, the blink of a witch going past on a broom.

A moment later, she landed on gravel in the alley behind Myrtle Street. Dorothy chose the narrow place carefully, between an old van covered in blue tarp and on her other side a plywood fence. She put her broom into her handbag—that was something The Great Marconi could only do with mirrors and sleight of hand—then she cinched her black coat and left gravel footprints around the parked van.

A crow called her from the chestnut tree and she acknowledged it with a nod. She was calm, as steady as her father visiting the president of the bank. Fearless. She was meeting Howard Plaid, the detective who was hunting her, head on.

A cat ran from her round the back of the garage. It racked the bluebells growing from the corner. Another cat heard them and watched her with wide yellow eyes. Dorothy smiled—Plaid had familiars and didn't even know it.

The kitchen light shined in the window upstairs. A pot was warming on the stove. Howard had glasses and pans full of water lined on the counter. The card hadn't lied, the water was really off. When he tried the faucet, it shook and hissed at him like a cobra. He quickly turned it off. There was nothing but anger in the pipes.

He was making coffee. He didn't know if Dorothy would want it. His own daughter never touched coffee. The water was beginning to bubble. When his daughter became a witch, she wouldn't even drink orange juice. Little things like that added up, until one day she was flying around the garden.

Dorothy stood before the door at the top of the stairs. All she had to do was knock.

Howard had decided on two cups.

He put a couple tablespoons of coffee crystals in each and reached for the hot pan. His hand didn't make it there.

The bubbles that formed in the boiling water were climbing like little balloons out of the pan and floating in the air. It had been a long time since he had seen magic in his kitchen. He reached and caught a bubble on the spoon. It was pearly, shiny, and rolled a little back and forth. And more of them whirled in slow orbit about him.

She knocked and they all shot back into the pan, turning into hot water again. He knew there was a witch at his door, he didn't have to wonder. He quickly poured, stirred, and left the cups steaming.

Although Dorothy had seen Howard in her crystal ball and last night too through a window, all he knew of her was a photograph her father gave him. That dark haired girl in the photo became a whole other person since going into the world on her own.

"I'm Dorothy Trillium."

He stepped aside and let her in. He had to push on the blue-white daylight to close the door. It felt like the morning wanted to follow her.

There wasn't much to his apartment and she stood in the middle of it like a Christmas tree.

"Oh," he said as he got her a chair "Here, have a seat. Sorry, I don't entertain much."

While she settled herself, he got the other chair from the table near the stove and carried it to the window next to her. "I used to live in the house," he explained. "Now I rent that out and I live here."

Her bright eyes stared past him at the army of water captured in pickling jars and pans. A full flower vase returned her glare.

Howard got a cigarette from his pocket. "They turned the water off this morning. Don't worry, this is all I've got. I filled the bathtub, but it all leaked out. The stopper's no good."

She smiled. "I'm not worried, Mr. Plaid." That was true, she had the confidence of a beekeeper. A witch had to.

A truck rumbled down the alley and all the water in glasses trembled and Howard saw a diamond of light run off her necklace and hide in her hair.

"I made some coffee if you like," he said. He put his unlit cigarette back in his pocket. He got up and walked to the sink.

"No thanks. No coffee for me. You probably knew that." Her voice knew he did.

"Yes. My daughter was the same way." He took a cup for himself.

"That's what interests me about you," she said. "Your daughter was a witch."

He sat across from her again. "That's right."

"And you work for the police."

He had a sip of coffee and swallowed and repeated, "That's right."

"And you saved the lives of those two witches yesterday."

Howard fumbled the cigarette from his pocket.

Dorothy said, "I find that interesting."

"You mind if I smoke?" Before she could answer he scolded himself, "No, that's okay. I'm trying to quit."

She could tell. There was a white half-shell on the windowsill. It was filled with ash and filters.

He said, "It hasn't been easy for me." The cigarette returned to his pocket. "It takes some getting used to. I'm sure you feel the same way."

"I'm doing okay," she said. "You can tell my father that. And tell him I flew over the old house a couple nights ago. I said hello. Tell him I'm fine, I like being a witch."

Howard nodded, "I'll tell him." He had some coffee. The taste agreed with him. Maybe he should make every cup with magic from now on. He looked for the diamond in her hair. It was still tucked away. "Your father was concerned about you. I bet he thinks about you every day."

She rolled her eyes.

"He said he has some very important news for you."

"I'm on my own now. This city is where I live. I'm learning to survive," she said, "I needed to find others like me. Magic has a way. It's funny, Mr. Plaid, I knew

we were going to meet. I believe we were meant to."
Then she surprised him, "Am I right to think you'd
like to see an end to witch hunting, Mr. Plaid?"

CHAPTER 6
The WITCH & the DETECTIVE

Howard Plaid steered the cardboard car onto Holly Street. When Dorothy told him that she flew a broom to his house, he insisted he drive her home. He didn't want to have her caught in the air if it started to rain. Gray clouds hovered over the islands.

They were still talking about the weather three blocks from Myrtle. She laughed and told him no, witches didn't listen to the weather reports. "They're crafty," she said, "Sometimes they predict sunshine just to catch you in a downpour."

That's when the car ran out of gas. They coasted to the curb.

Howard tapped the dashboard dial. "Empty." He drummed his fingers on the wheel. "Do you have a spell for this?"

"Do you want me to turn this into a horse and buggy?"

"Can you do that?"

She laughed. "I'm still pretty new to magic, Mr. Plaid."

"Well, that's alright. I don't mind walking." She didn't either, though she told him she could be home in two seconds on her broom. Time wasn't everything, every once in a while she would slow down and walk among ordinary lives.

The sidewalk rolled along. She pictured the streets when she was flying, and the town was like a map below her. She pointed out Taylor Avenue and said it was a shortcut, past the school into the wooded hills of the park.

The houses all looked half asleep lined up on either side. Some crows seemed to be following them. In the quiet between them, walking with a witch, Howard remembered a few years ago.

It wasn't an easy place to go. A night made frantic by hard rain and sirens. Howard drove a rocket car back then. He could be at the scene of the crime in less than a minute. It only took 13 seconds to reach Garden Street. Finding parking took longer. He went around the block three times before it happened. A yellow DeSoto, fat as a bee, bumbled away from the curb and Howard swept in. He cut the loud engine and the car stopped shaking. His hands were still trembling.

It was funny to know that in the future, that rocket car would end up under him in the garage, shadows climbing around it. It looked like it would never run again.

Grover Templin saw Howard approaching and ran to meet him. Blue and red police lights made him blink like pinball. "Detective!"

Howard raised a hand. This wasn't his call or anything, he just heard about the bust on the police band and came snooping. He sure didn't expect his world to be turned upside down.

The rain beaded on the rim of his hat and dripped. He heard a window break.

"Detective!" Behind Grover, a house was flooded with spotlights. "We got a nest!"

Howard was smoking a cigarette. Those were the days.

A big water truck parked on the lawn whined as it worked to empty itself into the house. Another window shattered. The police were throwing waterbombs. The firemen sprayed the walls. An arc of water hit the roof like a rainbow and made enough mist to put out Howard's cigarette.

"Are you lost in thought?"

Dorothy's voice brought Plaid back to the present. He realized where they were, on a sidewalk that turned into the driveway that wheeled into Mary Poppins Elementary.

"I guess I was," he said.

"Where were you?"

He was surprised he told her so easily, he didn't know he could. "I shouldn't have been there, the night my daughter died. When it was quiet, I'd get restless and run the police channel. That's how I heard about Garden Street." It would take the city half a century to apologize officially and set a marker there, where the house used to be.

"I didn't know my daughter was underneath all those lights and water. We thought we could keep her safe at home. She could fly around the garden on her broom and nobody had to know." He took his cigarette from the pocket where it had been sleeping. He mumbled around it, "Sorry..."

Grover Templin called it a nest. When they examined the remains, the cold wet clothes they dragged out of the house and lined up in the headlights on the lawn, they counted 16 girls' dresses and one that had fit a woman. That had been the teacher. Howard remembered her red and white striped socks.

"That was one of our schools," Dorothy said. She knew he was back there, that terrible night, seeing it again. He had the look of a man under a spell, walking in another world.

Howard recognized the button his daughter wore on her black overcoat. A purple umbrella. Then he realized he was looking at her small outline. All that was left of her was put in the rain. Her favorite pin gleamed like a jewel. He fell to his knees and in a quick scoop grabbed her clothes and stuffed them under his jacket. A last waterbomb went off and there were hollers from the house. Nobody noticed what Howard had done, too many shadows and blinking lights, it was easy for him to slip unseen through the crowd of uniforms, back under the yellow crime scene tape, over firehoses onto the sidewalk, between squad cars and trucks, into the people gathered on the street to watch the end of a witch's house.

That memory was real as a movie he might have seen a million times, where the actors were called back again and again to the same set and the roaring rain machine. Part of him was stuck to that reel of film, part of him heard crying and he stepped free.

Ahead of Howard, fifty feet or so, Dorothy kneeled on the sidewalk. A boy with an open mouth was crying like a baby bird. A girl his age stood beside him, crumpling her hands. Dorothy was soothing them with carefully chosen, warm sounding words.

By the time Howard arrived at their side, the boy was watching with shiny eyes as Dorothy held her hand out flat, just inches above something on the sidewalk. Her audience was mesmerized. Then, when she pulled her hand away, a frog was sitting there. It blinked and both kids jumped for joy. The boy caught it quickly before it could hop. The girl clapped her hands.

"See!" Dorothy told them, "It was only sleeping."

"What happened?" said Howard.

Dorothy watched them dance away with the frog that had known death for only a fleeting minute, and on its way to somewhere else, had been turned and returned. "Just a little magic," she said.

"You made it alive again?"

She touched a finger to her lips. She wasn't going to say.

That was okay. Howard had seen miracles before. Ahead of them, past the green playing field, bare winter trees scratched at the sky and stuck in their tangle, rising above like a birdhouse, was the water tower. He put his cigarette away for later and they headed that way.

A caw sounded like a car horn in the sky, then another. The crows were going there too. They perched on the catwalk and waited for the witch and the detective.

A couple times Howard got caught in branches and slipped on leaves, but Dorothy didn't have that problem, he even saw her walk through a tree. By the time they reached the water tower, Howard looked like he had fought his way through a Bowery Boys movie. Staring straight up at the steel peppered with black birds on top, he might have wondered how Dorothy meant to find her way inside. But, of course, she could fly. The crows greeted her on the railing.

And he fell once more into memory. Imagine

carrying all you have left of your child. Foot stomped on the rocket pedal, Howard made it home in seconds. That's where something really heartbreaking was waiting. When he told his wife the next morning it was too much for her. Their world was over. She took a rocket ship back to Mars. That was the last straw. He was left on planet Earth without her.

The crows all took off at once with the racket of a motorcycle gang.

Howard Plaid had that cigarette clamped in his mouth. He was dizzy from craning his neck and his right hand held a matchbook he was trying not to put to use.

Dorothy's broom brought her to the ground so quickly she seemed to have just popped beside him.

CHAPTER 7
SAMOVAR BETCH

Dorothy Trillium told Howard about a trail that would take him out of the park. She felt sorry about the briars that had torn his sleeves but it didn't matter because as soon as he could leave, he noticed his clothes had been to the laundry, mended and ironed and even his shoes had been shined somehow. Magic.

Behind him, the water tower got lost in the trees. He had been helping witches for years, as many as he could. For a while the authorities had let them be and Howard would only see witches on moonlit nights for a second. The last time it rained, he found a couple witches taking shelter in a parking garage. Since the war had resumed he tried his best to save each one. And he had to be a shadow about it, he had to act fast then be gone in the light.

Then something made Howard stop and listen. The faint drone of an airplane, songbirds, that low level rush of cars on a road, the presence of town breathing behind the alders. A detective had to develop these skills to feel through what only seemed to be reality. He stopped breathing when he heard it again…a flute, soft, but there like the creaking hinge of a shipwreck. It came from off the trail, beyond the sound of the creek, in one of those dark hollers songs are written about. Howard didn't seem to mind walking in the woods again. The twigs and holly leaves were glad to have him.

He paused at the edge of the creek to observe. The stream wasn't too wide, not much more than a bucket could pour from a mountain, but he didn't want to slip on the muddy other side. He didn't want to visit the Chief of Police looking like a mudguard. He could still smell the laundromat on his shirt collar as he took a deep breath and leaped.

It wasn't exactly flying, his shoes did slip a bit on the soft other shore, but his balance was good, there was nothing to be worried about. He held himself still and listened.

The flute drifted. It repeated the same eerie notes, three of them, then another. It could have been the call of a strange bird, one of those Martian ones that escaped from the zoo last summer. Too bad Howard gave away Otto Trillium's tiger food—if something with sharp teeth and claws was luring him, he might have to run.

Taking a step forward, a new sound chirped. The flute stopped. A shrill machine had begun to beep. The pulse quickened with each step Howard took in that direction.

Howard didn't look concerned anymore; he

recognized the trilling output of the police monitor. It was part of the witchfinder's arsenal. Rounding a thick hedge of devil's club, Howard surprised Samovar Betch.

"Plaid!" The witchfinder lowered his water gun. His hands were shaking. He hit the monitor switch and the steady squeal of it stopped. "I almost shot you!"

"What are you doing here?"

"Tracking a witch of course!" He examined dials on his machine. "Must be something screwy with the monitor…Unless you're packing magic."

"You think there's a witch out here?" Howard put on a good show looking about himself suspiciously.

"Some kid contacted me—thinks he saw a witch. He was bird watching, only caught a glimpse."

"Hmm…" Howard scanned what could be seen of the gray sky pieced between all the branches. "Could have been a crow."

"I know, I know. Most of the sightings are something perfectly explainable, but I check them out anyway. I thought I had one this time, you really had me going." He closed the lid of the scanner and sighed. "Looks like I'll have this recalibrated…" He heaved it off a tree stump and drew the strap over his shoulder. Falling into step with Howard, something suddenly occurred to Samovar, "Say, what are *you* doing out here? You're not trying to claim my witch, are you?"

"No," Howard lied, "I'm not. I'm just out here for my health."

"Yeah—I can't remember the last time you hooked a witch!"

"Yeah, yeah," Howard replied. He didn't mind the teasing, it meant the witchfinder didn't know.

Samovar chuckled, "Leave it to the professionals, Plaid."

A woodpecker backfired and Howard turned his head. It wasn't as simple as that to find a bird on a tree. "I heard a flute, was that part of your kit?"

"Hah!" Samovar dug into his thick jacket and showed the panpipes tied by cord around his neck. "Witches use these to communicate. All I need to do is set up a duck blind, blow on this thing and they come running."

"Really?"

"Sure." It was true that Samovar was weighted down with gear and tackle like some big-game hunter or someone fishing for marlin. A lot of it was junk, the stuff you could pick up at the Ben Franklin five and dime store—plastic witch dowsers, waterpaults, rain prisms, magic gum, spy eyeglasses, dollar gadgets and gizmos to detect or scare witches.

Somehow they were on a path again. Howard

didn't mind too much where it ended up. Samovar kept bragging about witch-finding and pretty soon a parking lot appeared between the trees.

"You need a ride?" Samovar offered when they reached the crackling gravel. A few cars were parked around but it was obvious which one was Samovar's. You didn't need a seeing-eye dog to find it.

Howard said, "No thanks." He wasn't about to go for a ride in a Plymouth with *Witch Exterminator* painted in gold calligraphy along the black finish. "This is a good day for walking."

Samovar pressed a button and his car squawked and threw open a door. "Not for me. I got places to go and if I don't get there fast, the witch flies the coop." He slung the monitor off his shoulder and placed it on the backseat. Before he shut the door, he got something off the floor.

"What's that?" Howard asked.

"Witch radar." Samovar stuck the magnetic base to the roof of his car. He grinned, "I got all the bells and whistles, buddy!"

"So I see."

The car squawked again, shutting the door for him and instantly opening the one on the driver's side. Samovar held up his opened hands and hissed, "Magic!" He laughed hoarsely as he got behind the wheel.

Howard counted seventeen red brooms painted on the door like the kills of a P-47. He could only hide his reaction by turning away. The car engine roared. Howard couldn't hear his shoes in the gravel.

Samovar called after him, "Say, where you walking to?"

"I'm going to the Chief's."

"What?"

Howard cupped his hands around his mouth, "The Chief!"

That brought more rasping laughter. Samovar snapped a halfhearted salute and spun the steering wheel with the other hand, then with a bang the rocket kicked him out of sight.

Howard shut his eyes, covered his face and turned his back a little late. The air was scorched, burned up like fireworks. He coughed. He lifted the sleeve of his coat and breathed that cloth. Smelling laundromat, he walked that way, like Count Dracula exiting the stage, off the parking lot.

Birds were singing again. The sidewalk was no trail in the woods, it was cement stuck beside a road. Still, Detective Plaid seemed to find interest in the sights. The neighborhood was just another walking attraction in a world stocked full of them.

This sidewalk, he noticed, was mottled with lichen, splotched as the hide of a gray dinosaur. He also noticed that this low world his shoes walked upon was just as full of drama. A shiny black beetle on its back kicked its legs. It was as tragic down there as a story on the front page of the *Herald*. Howard descended from the sky and with a giant finger, he tipped it over the way it was meant to be. It took a couple steps and over it went again. He had seen this happen before. Beetles seemed to reach a point in their life where it was just too much. Their legs tangled and tripped when they tried to continue. They rolled over on the sidewalk to die. "Okay," Howard said and stood. He hated to see it give up that way. A beetle ought to keep going until it turned to rust. So he left it twitching, waving like someone saying goodbye to a steamship disappearing on the Atlantic. The *Herald* would be appalled: **MAN ABANDONS BUG**.

He returned his attention to the houses on either side. He wasn't far from where he wanted to be. The address numbers kept rising on them like a thermometer.

Howard crossed the street and surprise, surprise, there was a table set on the sidewalk with a kid behind it in a wooden chair, arms crossed, looking like a miniature executive. A sign taped to the table interested Howard: COFFEE. He made eye contact and asked, "How much?"

"One American dollar." The boy's suit could have

fit a ventriloquist doll.

"A dollar seems a little steep."

"You won't find any better."

Howard scratched his chin. He missed out on his coffee this morning, all he had was a sip or two. He left the cup by the sink half full when he and Dorothy set out. Starting to reach for the dollar in his pocket, Howard paused, "What is it—Columbia roast?"

The kid answered automatically, "Sure." He got a paper cup and poured from a thermos. "The customer is always right," he piped.

"Yeah. Here you go," Howard gave the kid the dollar and took the hot cup of joe. "Get yourself a new bowtie." It looked like the sort that would spin or spit water if you got too close. Howard didn't take that chance, he quickly carried off his coffee.

He wasn't ten feet away when he spotted another table in his path ahead. Another kid too. Didn't they have school? Before he reached her, Howard waved.

She said, "You want some coffee, mister?"

"I just got some." He held up the cup so she could see.

She flashed a dimpled grin. "You'll be sorry then."

"Why?"

"Try it," she said.

Howard complied and immediately wished he hadn't. He spat it out and tossed the rest into the street.

The girl told him, "He doesn't know how to make coffee."

"You're telling me! It tastes like shoe polish."

"That's probably what it is. If you want coffee, *I* make the best on the block."

"I don't think so."

"Only a dollar twenty five," she continued and her dainty hands fluttered by the urn.

Howard pointed down the sidewalk. "*His* was only a dollar."

She raised her chin haughtily, "Mine's better. You pay for quality."

"No…" Howard shook his head, "I think I'm done with coffee for the day. I learned my lesson."

CHAPTER 8
HEXED

Samovar Betch had parked his car halfway over the curb in front of the Chief's house.

"Oh no…" Howard muttered. This didn't make his visit to the Chief any easier. He passed the fins and rocket nozzle ticking as it let off steam.

The windows of the Chief's house looked through iron burglar-proof bars, the door looked like a warhorse couldn't kick its way in. The grass on the lawn had been savagely cut to a crewcut length. It would prickle if you dared walk in bare feet. And planted in the center of the yard was a thick slice cut from a tree trunk, painted in red and white circles to be a target. An axe was stuck firmly in the bullseye. Howard followed the brick fortified path that led to the cement doorstep. All it lacked was a machinegun nest.

Before Howard could fathom how to announce himself short of starting an international incident, a metal slat parted on the door and a gruff voice demanded, "Who goes there?"

"Uhh…Detective Howard Plaid…Requesting permission to speak with the Chief."

The slat snapped shut, there was the sound of locks

85

unlatching, a series of clacks and scrapes, then the heavy door creaked open.

A familiar sandpapery laugh welcomed Detective Howard Plaid. "What took you so long?" Samovar Betch came into view, grinning with a carved expression.

"Wow…" Howard marveled. "A witchfinder *and* a butler."

Samovar ignored that remark. "Hey Chief!" he called over his should, "Plaid finally made it!"

"Wait a minute. This wasn't an appointment, I'm not late for anything."

"Sure, Plaid. You're not never late, you walk everywhere, or you drive a cardboard car. The world just waits for you to show up." Then Betch stepped aside, pushing the door open wide, as the Chief rolled into the gray daylight.

"Well, well, well," the Chief puffed. Even on a Saturday, the Chief wore his blue suit; it could be that it was bolted on to him with those silver buttons running up and down his sturdy uniform. "What brings you here, Detective Plaid? Are you going to tell me you discovered Witch Headquarters?"

Samovar cackled and the Chief growled, "Go make us some coffee, Sam."

"Yes sir. I will."

The Chief shifted his narrowed eyes back to his

latest visitor. "Sam tells me you ran into him in the park." He plowed out onto the doorstep like a bulldozer and Howard moved backwards out of the way.

"I took a shortcut," Howard explained. "Nevermind what he says, I wanted to talk to you in person. I went to see Otto Trillium yesterday."

The Chief crossed his arms over his barrel chest and studied the clouds to the west. For a postcard moment he was a bronze covered statue on a pedestal, then he spoke. "And what did you find out? Did you see his daughter?"

"She's not there anymore."

The Chief turned his head and broke free of being a statue. "Where is she?"

"I'm working on that..." said Howard. He felt the cigarette back in the corner of his mouth. The distance from his coat pocket was a well-traveled road, he didn't even know how it came and went.

The Chief sighed and dropped his arms so he could point. "You see that target, Plaid?"

"Yes sir."

"You ever throw an axe before?"

"No sir. I don't believe I have."

The Chief descended from the doorstep, said, "Follow me," and led Howard across the lawn towards the target. "I've been told it's very therapeutic."

The cropped lawn had the texture of a golf course.

Howard put a hand into his coat pocket and made a fist around an object in there.

The Chief snapped the axe from the target, felt the balanced weight of it like a 9-iron club, and said, "I'm told there's Zen in everything, even tossing an axe."

Together, they took twenty paces back from the scarred target.

The Chief paused, staring down the target with bull-like concentration, gathering tension in his arm. It must have been unnerving for the neighbors to watch every day.

Howard took a couple more paces away, to be clear of the windup and to be unseen by the Chief, as he took the witch's charm out of his pocket. Samovar Betch had been right when he detected magic on Howard in the woods, Dorothy had hidden it on him before they parted.

Behind the Chief, Howard opened his hand. On his palm sat a small ghostly bird.

The Chief raised his blue sleeve. The axe swerved back slowly the way a cobra will twist before it strikes, and Howard whispered a word.

Then a lot of things happened fast. Time needs to be slowed. Some observer with paper and pen, unaffected by the speed of time, separate from and impartial to the working of this world, would need to methodically write it down.

#1 The ghostly bird hovered off Howard's palm and aimed itself for the Chief.
#2 Samovar Betch reappeared in the doorway, carrying a tray with a coffee pot and cups. (He really could have been a butler).
#3 Samovar's wristwatch witch-detector alarm shrieked at the same instant he saw the unreal bird.
#4 The Chief was startled. The axe, already well into its forward swing was released too early.
#5 Samovar Betch let go of the coffee tray and reached for his gun.
#6 Howard Plaid saw the bird turn its wings.
#7 The first waterbullet was fired.
#8 The axe was flying way off target.
#9 A second waterbullet was fired.
#10 Howard heard the gunshots and began to drop.
#11 The Chief's arm followed through, crossing in front of him like a slow-motion pitcher, his eyes frozen on the deviating axe.
#12 A waterbullet wobbled like a bee just over Howard's head.
#13 The coffee tray hit the cement with a silver crash.

Time resumed its course. There was a bang as the axe hit the back tire of Samovar's rocket car. The magic bird had vanished. The waterbullet dissolved out of range across the street.

"Chief!" Samovar crunched over broken cups and kicked the urn. His butler duties were done.

The Chief stood with his back to both of them, rubbing his arm.

Loud crows left the top of a tree. A neighbor's door opened cautiously.

The alarm on Samovar's arm had quieted, he was just the sound of his shoes on the starchy grass. "Chief, you okay?"

"What in blue blazes just happened?" the Chief growled.

The hissing from the curb ceased as the last breath of air sighed from the punctured tire. The axe clanked next to the tipped Witch Exterminator.

Samovar gasped, "My car!"

"You numbskull!" the Chief roared, "Did you just discharge a weapon on my property? Twice?!"

"It was witchcraft, Chief! A hex!" Samovar stammered, "I was protecting you...What happened to my car?" The axe rested against it like a broken arm.

"Never interrupt a marksman!" the Chief thundered.

The two of them continued to sputter back and forth like a lawnmower pushed to the curb. Howard watched them and all he had to add was, "Therapeutic."

While the Chief tugged the axe and Samovar patted his car the way you would soothe a horse in need of a new shoe, Howard had nothing more to say.

He heard a train beyond them, a horn that told everyone it was passing through their town and didn't expect to be remembered. Who hangs to a bell after its rung? A car passed by, slowing for a second to gawk at the uniformed hulk holding an axe.

Howard managed to vanish like a magic act. If that bird was still around, it might have loaned him some ghostly power. But Dorothy knew what happened. She felt the bird give a last shriek before it died under a rhododendron.

She didn't need her crystal ball to picture Howard.

While she was thinking about him, he was thinking of her. He would have to tell her how he failed with her bird. That kind of apology didn't grow on trees.

His mind was busy and he wasn't expecting rain. A couple drops tested his skin, then more, then they dotted his suit like semaphore. All of a sudden it was pouring.

In his pocket he still had a Rain Tamer but there was no need to use it on himself. He didn't care if he got wet. He saved it for when he needed to help a witch. So he let the rain do its best. Each drop had a destiny. They were made up there and aimed by a bombardier. Howard Plaid happened to be their target.

A couple blocks over, he reconnected with Laurel Street and he got to the spot where he left his car and it wasn't there. Cars were constantly coming and going. There was a Mercury and a Toyota where his car should have been. It was too wet to worry about it now, he would come back later. Hooligans would sometimes pick up cardboard cars and move them. It was a whole phenomenon. Once he found his car in a sturdy tree. That was no fun getting it down. He squinted his eyes, looked around and gave up. It was out of gas anyway. What could anyone do, use it for a paperweight? Might as well let it go until tomorrow. The rain slanted in the streetlights the way an artist will brush charcoal across the paper.

Who knows how many steps he took in all that splashing until he finally climbed the stairs to his room? Beside the telephone the answering machine light was blinking. He pressed the button and heard an unhappy voice. She wasn't from Mars or a water tower in the park.

"I just received a call from this number and they were asking me about my age and about my Medicare and they hung up on me and I call back and I found out it isn't even anything that has to do with Medicare. Please don't call me again."

Who knows who that was? There were phantoms in his room and phantoms in the phoneline. A witch must be on the way. He took off his cold coat and dropped it over the chair. He saw his coffee waiting by the sink and thought how that would be nice when it was hot again, but just then the phone started to ring. A picture formed in his mind and he knew it wasn't someone angry. He cradled the receiver to his ear and said, "Hello, it's me, Howard."

Her voice was like its own animal circling him, "Hi Howard. It's me, Dorothy."

He knew it. The curtains covered the window. He looked like he remembered everything all over again. "Hello, Dorothy," he said, as if it was simple as can be to travel to him in the air. "I just got back…Yeah, I went to see the Chief. The bird didn't work…I don't know what happened, I don't know what I did wrong."

The telephone poured sand between his ears back and forth. A desert. He waited in the middle of it for an answer. Bedouins crossed the dunes, a wave of heat shimmered like smog.

His kitchen was still filled with emergency water. It seemed overkill. If the faucet didn't work, he could hold a cup out the window and in a minute it would be full.

Dorothy had seen it all in her crystal ball. Her room in the water tower was lit by candles. Cathedral shadows crept up the wall.

"Don't worry," she said, "We can try again."

She could see the next time they would be together, tomorrow, after the rain.

"And that's not all," he continued. "I lost my car. It's not where we left it. I hope it hasn't turned to mush in the rain."

"Hold on, let me see." She set her phone down and went to the table to get her crystal ball. She could see everything with that magic eye.

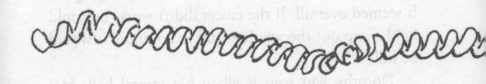

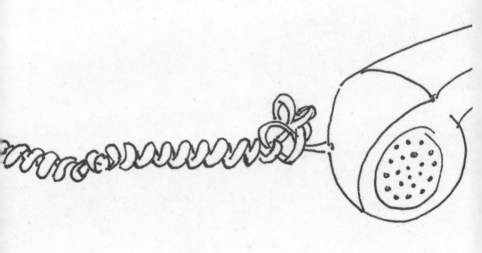

CHAPTER 9
A GIRL from PARIS

Howard Plaid knew that Dorothy was nearby. Every dish and cup of water was humming like a glass harmonica. A picture on the wall was swinging from its nail. So he left the kitchen and went outside to meet her.

He didn't see her at first, not on the landing or on the stairs but he knew she was somewhere. His daughter used to be able to turn herself in the air so she could be almost invisible. What a laugh she would have as she called his name. "Dorothy?"

Her answer wasn't a sound he could hear, she made a picture in his mind like a dream of where she was. His daughter used to do that too. He went down the stairway and around the corner to find her in the garden.

"Your wife planted a lot of Martian flowers."

"She tried," he said. "They all died."

"That's what you think." Dorothy ran her hand above the ground. There wasn't much there to look at but some broken down weeds and a thistle and some things that had long since bloomed. Howard didn't give the garden much attention. "Come here," Dorothy said. "Look."

Witches were enchanting. They could make you see things, they could make you forget the things you thought you knew. When Howard stood beside Dorothy, the ground began to scribble and pulse. All the seeds needed was a witch to tell them what to do. They grew fast as a wave coming in around her legs. Tall stalks, colored like crayons, leaves and vines that unfurled and flowers big as hubcaps. They spun like a parade of Cadillacs carrying astronauts. A low hum came from them.

"What are these?" said Howard.

"They're called telephone flowers," Dorothy said. She touched the petals of one and there in the round center a picture formed...An orange desert, a green sky, a little blue house shaped like a bowler hat with a garden of similar flowers.

Howard leaned over the view as it moved in a Martian breeze. "I know this place!" He ought to, there was a painting of it on the wall by the kitchen cupboard. The scene in the flower was that same watercolor. He put his hands beneath the bowl of petals. "What do I do? Is this really a telephone? Can I talk to her?"

Dorothy said, "You can send her a message," and she showed him how to make words. Martians used flowers to communicate, as if gardens were typewriters planted in rows.

It took him a minute to think of what to say, it had to be simple, it had to be direct, he needed her to know who it was right away. He settled on seven letters and as he pressed the keys, he saw the word appear spelled in bright flowers in the garden in front of her Martian house. He held onto the telephone flower after he was done, liking the rosy glow of the hello he formed, then he let go and the stem sprung back. Like the steady drone of a dial tone, his message was done.

Other flowers had other pictures, but he said all he wanted to, to the only one on Mars he knew. He stepped out of the garden, back onto the flagstones, careful of where the aqueduct ran.

As Dorothy followed him, the wave of flowers fluttered like the pages of a telephone book and whirlpooled through the topsoil into the network of the dark unmapped world hidden underground.

Not a cable was left, the backyard garden looked the same as before, when contact with Mars was just science fiction.

Howard said, "When I met Miranda, I didn't know where she was from. I listened to her and for some reason I thought she was a girl from Paris. It was the way she talked, or the way she looked, I guess. I knew she wasn't from around here," he almost laughed.

"That's why you wrote Bonjour."

"Yeah. She'll know that was me reaching out." He turned around and looked at where the flowers had been. "Will they come back if she has something to tell me?"

"We'll see...Witches and Martians aren't so very different. We have to keep our magic secret."

"Yeah," he sighed. "I guess you're right."

"But I did find your car...I can take you there, it's not far."

He already had on his coat and fedora. "Okay," he said, "why not?" He couldn't just stand there beside the arch of the miniature aqueduct and stare at the weeds, waiting for a Martian flower to appear. Not when he had a witch who came all this way to help him. "Let's go."

It was true, it really wasn't that far. The thieves or pranksters who picked up his car only moved it across the street from where Howard parked it, into the broad lot of Food Giant. He couldn't see it yet, but Dorothy told him it was in there, hidden by hoods and roofs and fins.

"Sorry about the bird," Howard muttered.

"That's okay."

"I didn't know if I was supposed to throw it at the Chief or let it find its own way." He hovered one hand above the other, "It flew off my hand and then with the gunshots it was gone."

Dorothy shrugged, "I took a chance letting you try. Not everyone can do magic right away."

They waited for the traffic light. "We can try something else," she said, dropping her voice, "There are other spells."

"What would that bird have done to him?" Howard said, a notch above a whisper.

She smiled. "It wasn't really a bird. It was an idea. It would have made him think differently. A thought can be powerful magic." When she blinked, the traffic light changed. That could have been magic too, or just a machine timed to do that. She was still smiling as they crossed the street.

Nine huge letters spelled FOOD GIANT in the air. With the red neon shining in them at night, the rooftop would glow and every moth for blocks would show to fill up shopping carts with light. The butcher took their orders, cutting slices of phosphorous. Paper bags just big enough to carry in their feathered hands as they flapped home.

A parking lot could be rolled up tight and hung in the sky—it's not much more than a beehive, a place where cars buzz in and leave. Most people don't find them that exciting. Put another way, you won't find postcards being sold of your favorite parking lot. Pilgrims and tour buses weren't coming to Food Giant to marvel at the tar, or if they were, they were part of a secret society steeped in mystery. Witches, detectives, and The International Order of Parking Lot Attendants would all search for signs and wonders among the cars.

"Dorothy pointed, "There it is!"

"Where?" He followed her finger, but he didn't see it. "It's a blue Chrysler Cardshark..." Then he groaned, "Ohhh," as he spotted it. His car had gone lopsided, the cardboard sides were melted like a candle. "The rain got it."

Taped to each side was a notice—white paper, black typed letters—when they were close enough, they could read:

WARNING. Your vehicle must be removed from the Food Giant parking lot. If not moved by 12/10 it will be towed. This is your one and only warning. Thank you. The Food Giant Management.

Dorothy let out a breath, "Yikes! That sounds a lot like a curse." She picked at the tape and took the sign off the back window. While she moved about the car removing the other three notices, Howard scratched at the damp cardboard latch on the roof. When it was in perfect working order, the car could fold like origami. But it took some work and effort to fold into a two-dimensional slice of car that he rolled between her and himself like a bicycle. The four wheels pressed together wobbled. He held a soggy crease. As they passed a green garbage bin, Dorothy threw the crumpled curse in.

Retracing their steps, they returned to the corner, only Howard, pushing a squeaking cardboard wall, didn't notice the woman standing by the telephone pole until she spoke to them.

"Have you been to the 99 Cent Store today?" Considering the clothes she wore, it was surprising she didn't glow right through Howard's cardboard. Baggy pink sweatpants, a bright red parka, lime green tennis shoes, long hair dyed orange, topped by a turquoise knit cap. She reached into her *Herald* newspaper shoulder bag and deftly plucked out two yellow flyers. She stuck her arm around Howard's shield and grinned, "Take one. We have lots of good deals today. Everything in the store is 99 cents." She gave one to Dorothy too, "Here you go, honey," adding conspiratorially, "No expiration date."

Howard scanned the paper he held. Bold lettering at the top announced UNDER NEW MANAGEMENT. And: *1000s of Items To Select From. No Games, No Gimmicks Just! 99¢ or under.* Howard's eyes stuck on: *Best Buy Cigarettes 89¢.* The one in his coat pocket had seen better days. He thought of it, as he heard Dorothy's voice.

"Oh…I think you gave me something else by accident."

There was actual surprise in the woman's face as she accepted the flyer sized photo from Dorothy. "This is my dog!" she cried, "This is Ping Pong!" A light had clicked in her like those big neon bulbs in the Food Giant sign and she beamed on the sidewalk, "How'd you do that?"

"I don't know," Dorothy hid her harmless lie in a smile, "It must have been in with your flyers."

"I love it!"

Howard watched from over his folded fence of a car.

"You know what I'm going to do?" she asked Dorothy. "I'm going to go to the 99¢ store and get a quality frame to put this in!"

"Okay!" Dorothy laughed.

"Bye bye!"

Dorothy said, "Au revoir!" and waved.

Howard stuffed his flyer in a pocket so he could hold his car with both hands. "That was a pretty piece of magic," he said. A bicycle rang bells beside them in the street. "How did you manage that trick?"

"It was no trick," she said. "I can tell what people are missing."

"Can you?" He rolled the car forward an inch, ready

to bump it down the curb whenever the crosswalk light decided to change. "What about me?"

She glanced at the sky, she always had to keep an eye on the weather, and then her eyes returned to his. "I can tell you miss your daughter and I know you miss your wife. You have a broken heart, Mr. Plaid. And that's not something you can replace at the 99¢ store."

A rocket car roared by close, a hot wind and reek of kerosene, and Howard held on tightly to the pitching cardboard sail. It almost got away from him, it was like hauling in a fishing net. When he could rest it back on its wheels, there was no sign of Dorothy, she had vanished with the breeze.

CHAPTER 10
The ROCKET CAR

Dorothy Trillium could tell the rocket car was on the way and she knew who was behind the wheel. Every witch had heard about Samovar Betch—like the crocodile in *Peter Pan*, he was loudly ticking, not difficult to avoid if you didn't panic. As soon as Dorothy felt the presence of the car radar, she reached for her broom. There was enough time in a second for her to tell Howard goodbye, even though she knew her voice would be lost in the rocket as she rode the broom over the top of the apartments.

Howard guessed that loud blast of a passing car was Samovar Betch in the Witch Exterminator. That would explain why Dorothy turned into air. All Samovar caught was a blip on the dashboard detector. It could have been anything—a pigeon or a strong prayer.

The water was still off. Howard supposed that meant she would be back. She wouldn't return if water was able to throw her off guard. He filled a pan with the day-old water from a flower vase and turned the burner on.

His cardboard car leaned against the wall like a Roman coin. It just needed time to dry.

The room felt lonely. He wanted to hear Dorothy, but he picked up the phone and dialed another number. Outside, a crow was being radio. "Hello," he said when the ringing stopped, "Is this Mr. Trillium?"

"Yes."

"This is Howard Plaid."

"Yes, the detective I hired. Any news to report? Have you done your job and found my daughter?"

Howard toyed with the frayed cigarette. "No. I haven't found her yet. I met a witch who knows her though."

"She's running into other witches who knows where?" her father cried. "This is exactly what I was afraid of, Mr. Plaid! I hired you to protect her! I hired you to get her back before bad things happen!"

"This other witch assured me Dorothy is fine. She is taking care of herself. She's stronger than you think, Mr. Trillium."

"Do you realize all it takes is one cop with a water pistol, or a bucket of water thrown by a lunatic and my daughter is done? I want her home, Plaid. It's already been too long. If you can't find her, I'll get someone else who can. Witchfinders are a dime a dozen in this town."

Trillium ended the call and Howard held a dead receiver in one hand and a crushed cigarette in the other. The paper of it was unraveling. Tobacco flakes flecked his fingertips.

Then the phantoms reappeared in his room. The rocking chair started to move. A book flipped open and pages riffled. Peculiar dots of light danced on the floor. A witch was near...he went to open the door.

"Hi Dorothy," he greeted her.

"Hi. Can I come in? I won't stay long, I have a spell brewing at home."

"Of course." He made room for her.

"Sorry I left you like that. Without you hearing me say goodbye, I mean. That guy in the rocket car is bad news."

"Samovar Betch."

"That's him. I've learned to avoid him. He only preys on the younger ones, the sick and the very old."

"Yeah," Howard answered, "I know him." They took seats, Dorothy in the rocking chair and Howard by the window. He looked troubled. "Someone like that, doing what he does, murdering...I'm surprised...I guess I'm surprised you haven't rubbed him out."

She shook her head. "No. We're not capable of using our powers to injure."

"Really?"

She nodded.

He stared at the tobacco dust on his fingers. If he had the magic to turn the relics into a cigarette, he would. "Then why are the police making war?"

"You tell me," she said.

"I don't think they know anything about witches. My daughter was never wicked with her magic." He noticed there were no more crumbles on his fingers, he would need a telescope to search the floor for where they landed. "All people need to know is the truth."

"That spell I gave you for the Chief was supposed to do that. He would have snapped out of his delirium, he would have given orders for a ceasefire. He would be ready for witches to be living here. Maybe wishful thinking takes more than a magic spell."

"I should be able to think of some way to tell everyone…I could write a letter to the *Herald*. With any luck it would be a frontpage story. **GUMSHOE GOES ROGUE**."

That made her laugh. She could picture the sidewalk vending machines. She could hear the kid on the corner hawking copies. "It would be a start."

"Yeah, right…Say would you like a coffee—or no—a tea?"

"I'm okay."

"Well, I've got all these pans of water. I don't know when the faucets will work again, but I could use a coffee." He headed for the kitchen and passed the telephone. "Oh gee—" he stopped, "I should tell you—just before you got here, I talked to your father on the phone." He went the last few steps to the stove and lit the burner. She still hadn't answered him. "I didn't tell him you found me. I said I met a witch who told me you were fine."

"I'm not going back there."

"Yeah, that's what I tried to tell him." Howard dipped a spoon into the jar of coffee crystals. "He's set on getting you back though, he needs to talk to you." Howard shoveled a small mound into his cup. "He told me he would hire a witchfinder if I didn't bring you back."

"Oh brother…"

"I know…" Howard looked at the water in the pan. Some bubbles began to form.

"I'm not going back," she repeated.

"Yeah…" Howard had the bent cigarette, his last cigarette, waiting for a match. It didn't seem right for it to fall apart when it could be breathed in and out for as long as it took to die. Still, he seemed startled to find the cigarette in his mouth again and he put it away before he spoke. "Maybe you could invite your father to the water tower so he could see that you're okay?"

"I don't think so. He'll show up with a cage to catch me in."

Howard took a moment to prepare his coffee. The spoon sang as it spun.

"Anyway, Mr. Plaid, I just stopped by to say a

proper goodbye for now. I need to get back to the tower and I'll have to think of what to do about my dad. Thank you for your help…it would be nice if we could uncomplicate everything."

While he led her to the door, he left his coffee by the sink. By the time he saw it again, it would be no warmer than the waters corralled around it.

Howard opened the door to pouring rain. It was like damp dynamite.

Dorothy scrambled backwards as he slammed the door shut.

"I'm sorry! I had no idea it was raining!" But now Howard could hear it peppering the roof, he just hadn't been listening before. In the winter, the rain could fall at any moment from skies that stayed gray for months. "Weatherwise, this town is a terrible place for witches to be."

"I know," she agreed. "We should live somewhere dry like the desert…or on Mars. But I have to get back to my cauldron somehow. It's too bad I don't have the spell to make your car work in the rain. There's not much a witch can do in the rain."

"Well…I do have another car. I keep my old rocket car in the garage downstairs. It's been years since it drove. I'm not sure if it will work anymore but we can try."

"It's worth a try. I don't want to dodge raindrops

all the way home, it's exhausting and painful."

Another door at the back of the room opened to a steep set of stairs. Howard turned on a light and the gloom turned into sharp-looking shadows. Up high, a spider marked time catching dust in its web. "Careful on the steps," he said. Her shoes clacked behind him to the ground floor.

The clutter of the garage surrounded a silent rocket car. Half covered in a patchwork blanket of tarps, it looked fast asleep. It looked as if it had been that way since 1953. "Hard to believe, isn't it?"

"It certainly is." Dorothy ran a finger over the dusty fin.

With a loud crackling, Howard removed the tarp, knocking over a coffee can that rolled and left a trail of oil. There was more rust and dents then he remembered. When he turned the door handle the hinges creaked reluctantly and he needed both hands to open it. "There we are," he said at last. He coughed. It smelled like a mummy's tomb. "It would help if you had some herbs or something to burn, sage or hemlock or whatever."

"As long as this car keeps the rain out."

"Oh sure, this old car is airtight as a canteen." He crawled in behind the wheel and adjusted the ragged afghan blanket that was thrown over the cracked vinyl bench seat. "Welcome aboard."

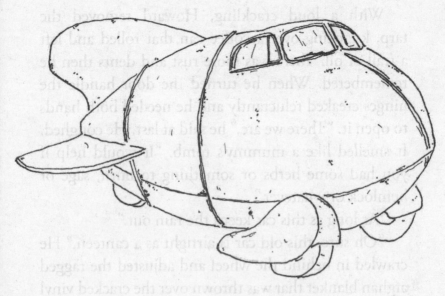

Dorothy said, "Thanks" and got inside beside him. As soon as she succeeded in shutting the door, she dug through her handbag and took out a tied bunch of dried flowers. She waved it like incense then placed the bundle on the dashboard.

"Yeah," Howard nodded. "That's much better. What is that, Mummy-Be-Gone?"

"Something like that," she smiled.

"Well, I must have known this day was coming—look, I left the key in the ignition. Now, if you've got another spell for starting a car, this would be the time."

CHAPTER 11
The BIG CROW

CHAPTER II

THE BIOGRAPHY

Howard Plaid's rocket car took 45 seconds to reach the parking lot closest to Dorothy's water tower. The engine gave a last rattle and they tried to see what lay ahead through the steamed glass. A dark silhouette against a silver sky.

"Oh no…" Dorothy leaned closer to the windscreen and wiped at the condensation.

"What's the matter?" Howard gave the windshield wipers a flick.

"Look!"

Howard couldn't believe what he was looking at. The water tower was covered in slick black feathers.

"We're too late," Dorothy groaned. "I have to get up there before anyone sees. Before it gets worse."

"Worse?"

She looked him in the eyes. "How would you like a hundred foot crow flying around town?"

He cleared the windshield rain again and it looked like the water tower supports were already turning into legs. "No, I wouldn't. How do we stop it? How do we get you up there safely?"

"There's only one sure way. You'll have to carry me."

"Carry you? How am I going to climb up there holding you?"

She rolled her eyes and reminded him, "Magic." She opened her bag, looked in there quickly and removed her broom. "You just hold onto this and it will take us to the top."

"Where will you be while this is happening? It's pouring out there."

Dorothy handed him the broom. "I'll be in here, in your pocket. Now hurry!"

She didn't let him argue, she was already where she wanted to be, he could feel her next to that last cigarette, and he was holding the broom. "Okay... Okay, here we go," he said. He slid across the empty car seat and opened the door. Outside was a world of rain.

He stood in a puddle looking up through the falling rain at the biggest bird he'd ever seen. A wing dragged itself free of its round body. He addressed the girl in his pocket, "Just so you know, I've never flown a broom before. Do I—?"

In the next wet moment, he was standing on the catwalk a hundred feet in the air. His free hand seemed guided as it reached into the breathing feathers and opened a hatch. He had to time it right, between the enormous breaths so he could get through the gap in one leap.

It may have been turning into a bird on the outside, but inside it was still her room. He imagined it could have been most any young woman's apartment except that it was in a water tower rapidly turning into a crow and there was a bubbling cauldron in the center.

She was quick as lightning to leave his pocket and find her size and track across the room to where her spell was smoking and sparking.

The floor tipped up then down as a clawed foot spread out in the grass. If there were birdwatchers out there in the rain, they wouldn't need binoculars. Another minute and everyone would see the monstrous crow blot above town.

Dorothy worked to make sure that wouldn't happen—adding ingredients to the recipe, stirring the cauldron with a wooden spoon until the fuming clouds dispelled. A shudder rocked the room. Dorothy whispered something, ran her hands over the cauldron, and it was clear of whatever was troubling it.

Howard, who had drifted forward carrying her broom, was drawn to look in the cauldron. "It's empty," he said. It was true. That cauldron was smooth as a new bowl. "You did it."

"That was close...Another minute and we would've been airborne." She waved the wooden spoon and he noticed the black feathers pinned to it. "Speaking of which..." She plucked a feather off the spoon, "Here's your ticket back to the ground."

"A crow feather?" It was a lot less than a jet-pack or a parachute.

"This is magic. All you need to do is hold it and when you step off the catwalk you will float down."

Howard tried out the sentence, "Hold onto a feather, step off the catwalk and float to the ground." He didn't like it. He knew he was in the presence of witchcraft, but his expression couldn't lie. He sighed. "No ladder, huh?"

"No, the ladder welds broke long ago. The rest of it rusted away."

Howard soured.

"I'm sorry I can't fly you to the ground on my broom but it's still raining and I have to be alone to prepare more spells."

He looked at the feather resting across his open hand.

"You can trust me, Mr. Plaid."

"Yeah, I know." He rolled the white quill tip between his fingers then held it still, angled out from him like an airplane wing. "Feather, catwalk, jump…"

He turned around when he got to the hatch. Dorothy was busy gathering ingredients from drawers, but she pulled her hood about her face before he opened the latch. Funny she had so many powers, but the smallest raindrop could do her in.

"So long, Dorothy."

"Don't worry, Mr. Plaid."

He opened the door to the wind and rain. He went through quickly onto the same old catwalk and not a single crow feather remained on it.

When he took a step towards the railing, he heard the metal slats beneath his feet creak. Every pound of him was about to fall and he didn't like it. He took a deep breath and avoided looking at the ground. He chose a spot in the clouds to concentrate on. The wind moved it like a ghost curling and rolling. He was getting wet waiting. He reminded himself when the Great Wallendas were this high in the air, they weren't scared.

Clutching that crow feather, Howard made his shoe lead him off the catwalk. If it wouldn't work, what could he do? There would only be a couple seconds to remember Mars and witches.

Earlier in winter the maple trees let the breeze scatter their whirlybird seeds. They twirled like helicopters over the street and sidewalks and lawns. That's how Howard Plaid descended, as if he rode on a carrousel slowly obeying gravity.

It wasn't until he landed that he realized he had been holding his breath the entire ride and the feather was nearly crushed in his fist. That was okay, he only needed a one-way ticket. His right shoe was placed ankle deep in a puddle, but he didn't seem to mind. His clothes were soaked, the rain ran down his face and his hands were cramped and cold but none of that mattered—he was stunned to still be alive. He didn't expect Dorothy to be on the balcony when he looked up there and he bit his lip as if there was something he couldn't say. It would have to wait. For now he had to get out of a puddle.

The rocket car would be dry. He rubbed his stinging eyes and felt his wet hair. How nice it would be to sit behind the wheel with all the heater vents blowing. That would have to wait, first he had to find his fedora hat. The wind had taken it off and hidden it somewhere in the brush. It wasn't anywhere obvious. A fedora was no ordinary leaf to be lost in the woods.

After a few minutes of searching during which he became as soaked as a seaweed farmer, Howard's mud-covered shoes squelched on a deer-path lined with kelpish elderberry and salal when suddenly he spied his hat resting on top of a rhododendron.

Howard pressed against the branches and stretched for it. Just as he touched the brim, it gave a yelp. For a second it seemed to be more magic, something Dorothy might have left him with for a laugh—a talking hat!—but then it levitated and Howard was met by the boy underneath it, wearing it.

"I'll be darned..." Howard said. "You found my

hat."

The boy pushed the hat back so he could see—it was big enough that it slid about on him all too easily.

"What are you doing out in the rain?" said Howard.

"I'm a birdwatcher," the boy said. He wore binoculars around his neck. Then he corrected himself, "I mean I used to be a birdwatcher," and he pointed at the looming water tower. He had a good view of it from his hiding place. "Now I'm a witchwatcher." His eyes disappeared under the fedora again and he thumbed it back. "Are you a witch too? I saw you fly down from there."

"No. I'm not a witch, I'm a detective." Howard reached in his coat, past the pocket where that cigarette tempted him, and he showed the kid his badge. "I've been working with that witch. On a top-secret case. You haven't told anyone about her, have you?"

"Not since I came back. The first time I saw her, I did. I called that guy on the TV commercials, the Witch Exterminator, but he didn't even give me a reward. He didn't believe me."

"Listen, kid. I believe you. You're right. But I can't let you tell anyone what you've seen. Can you keep this a secret, please?"

If Howard Plaid really sold umbrellas door to door, he would have seen that boy's expression before—it was the hard sell—and he had to think of something quick. "What if I let you keep my hat? It's the genuine detective article. It's been in gang busts and car chases and once it even saved me from a gunshot. You can still see where the bullet grazed it. If I wasn't wearing that hat, I would've been dead. Now it can protect you. It can be yours if you promise to keep a detective's secret."

"Well...I *do* like it."

"Sure you do! It looks good on you too. You look like a brother shamus."

The boy smiled.

"So what do you say?" Howard waited.

"I'll keep it," he decided. "And I'll keep your secret too. Us detectives got to stick together."

"Yeah, that's right!" Howard laughed, relieved. The rain didn't bother him. He could get another hat like that at Woolworths. He didn't really believe that fedora had been keeping him alive. That was just superstition. He made a salute against his wet forehead but as he was starting to leave, the kid called out to him.

"Say, mister! Was that tower really turning into a bird, or was I seeing things?"

Howard paused. "Being a birdwatcher, you've seen a lot of different birds, right?"

The boy nodded and corrected his hat.

"Have you ever heard of a bird as big as a water tower?"

"No…"

Howard pointed, "Does it *look* like a bird?"

The kid shook his head, no.

"Then I'd say it's safe to assume you were just seeing things."

CHAPTER 12
WHEN the CITY WAKES UP

Sunny Jim's dog was old, 16, equivalent to 112 in human years. It tottered when it walked out in the yard where it seemed a gust would lay it flat. Cataract eyes, hair that bristled in unkempt swatches like unbaling hay, feeble jutting bones that it moved uncertainly with the staggered jerks of a tangled marionette.

But Sunny Jim loved his pet. He would wait in the doorway then lift it over the step when it was ready to come back inside the house.

He didn't know how much longer this routine would last...he hoped that he and his dog in their quiet unassuming way had found eternity.

But someone had plans for them.

That plan began with a yellow card.

It fell through the maildrop a couple days ago. Sunny Jim rescued it from his dog's mouth and read what was left of it:

NOTICE !

ater service will be interrupted

S	M	T	(W)	TH	F	S

from **7:30 am** to **6:00 pm**

on **11·04·2020**

for repairs to system

EPARTMENT OF PUBLIC WORKS
PHONE (360) 778.7700

\Administration\Operations\Admin\Master Forms\Water

The first thing Sunny Jim did was check his house for witches. He didn't have to be a rocket scientist to know what was going on. Sunny Jim listened to the news. Just this week, he heard about a man who caught witches in his basement. And that happened after the guy got a notice from the Water Department too. It was common knowledge that witches wouldn't enter a house with running water.

So Sunny Jim had been on edge for days while his water stayed turned off. He carried a water pistol, he jumped at shadows and omens. He was sure a witch had him in her sights...He had to stay on his toes.

When he let Oscar outside in the morning, he felt like an outlaw in a Western as he checked the street, the parking lot, the yards on either side, the sky. He puffed on a cigarette nervously. Oscar creaked across the rugged winter lawn. Sunny Jim blew a cloud at the crow on a wire.

A spoon fell onto the floor in the kitchen. The sound carried like a bell through the house to the open door where Sunny Jim gave a jump. Oscar didn't hear it, the ancient dog was half taxidermied, it wasn't really in our world anymore. It was pointed into the wind.

Sunny Jim had his gun drawn and he ran inside, ready for a rain of waterbullets. He almost shot his TV as his reflected image flashed across the dull screen. He slid into the kitchen on one knee with his pistol taking aim at everything. Nothing that wasn't there before, the sink, the water stacked on the counter, the table with the ashtray, the *Herald*, a dish with a poached egg. But there was a spoon on the linoleum tile. Sunny Jim kept the gun pointed at it as he approached. Why couldn't a witch turn into a spoon? What better disguise in a kitchen?

While Sunny Jim crept towards it, outside in the yard Oscar rose off the ground, floated over the picket fence, and popped out of sight.

"I see you," said Sunny Jim in what he hoped was a good George Raft imitation. "If you're a spoon, turn back into a witch or I'll let you have it." His hand was shaking, wrapped tightly around the gun. Then he pulled the trigger. It took three shots to hit. Nothing happened. No drowned witch suddenly appeared on the floor. It was just a spoon.

Ash fell off his cigarette.

The clock ticked loudly on the wall.

He picked up the spoon and put it on the counter. The daily suspense was getting to him. Fooled by a spoon...

After a fright like that, a gunfighter wouldn't just put his gun away and leave the kitchen and cross the open space of the living room back to the front door, but Sunny Jim let his guard down. He was thinking about the dog. Oscar would stand still as a museum animal until Sunny Jim came to get his old friend.

But his dog wasn't there. "Oscar!" Sunny Jim stood in the doorway and clapped his hands sharply. His deaf dog could sense that disturbance in the air the way a dragonfly resting on a cattail stem will feel the vibration when a frog hops into the pond. "Oscar!"

Sunny Jim stepped outdoors. This was why he wore slippers. He took Oscar outside several times a day, no point in getting cold feet. There was no sign of the dog. The yard wasn't that big and Oscar couldn't climb the tree. "Oscar?" The gate was shut, there weren't any fence slats knocked down. Poor Sunny Jim didn't know what to do…He ran it round his mind like a tornado. It was a terrible dream he couldn't wake from. He called the only detective he knew.

Howard Plaid was soaking wet as he opened his apartment door and hurried to the ringing phone. He took off his coat on the way and let it slap on the floor. "Hello?" If he was expecting Dorothy checking up on him, he was wrong.

"This Howard? This here is Sunny Jim."

A crooked line or two creased his forehead. "Yeah?" He carried the phone over to the stove and poured his cup of cold coffee into a pan. "What do you want? You in trouble again?"

"Trouble just seems to follow me," Sunny Jim sighed. "I can't find my dog."

Howard adjusted the blue flame of the burner. "Did you call the dogcatcher?" The lines of his forehead appeared around his mouth as he smiled. He didn't want to be cruel, but it had been a long day and he didn't want to catch pneumonia looking for Sunny Jim's raggedy dog and he couldn't even take a hot shower.

"You gotta help me find him."

"I'm not sure if—"

Sunny Jim interrupted him, "You still a detective, ain't you?"

"Yes. I'm still a detective, but I'm on another case right now. Two actually." He scratched his wet hair, "Three?" His mind was preoccupied with that: The Chief, Otto Trillium, Dorothy…Yeah, that made three.

"Howard, you there?"

"Yeah. I'm sorry, I've got my hands full. I'm working for three different clients right now. You could try the dogcatcher though. Maybe he was lonely."

"Listen, Howard. This ain't no laughing matter. It's witchcraft!"

Howard stopped the movie playing in his head of a dog sitting on the front seat of an Animal Prevention cab. With just one word, Sunny Jim just became his fourth client. "Witchcraft?" While Howard listened to the explanation, he thought about Dorothy. He remembered she had a crystal ball. He could call her and ask if she could tune in Oscar.

"And that's why I called you," Sunny Jim finished. The receiver was silent for a few seconds. "You there, Howard?"

"Yeah, yeah. I just had an idea. Let me see what I can do. Give me a call later." He ended their conversation and let the long telephone cord pull him back to the table. The answering machine's red message light was blinking. He replaced the phone in its cradle and pressed the PLAY button. Maybe it was from Mars or Dorothy. The coffee was burning.

BEEP. A robot announced, "Sunday, 7:47 AM." Then the message began.

"I hope you said this was the Henderson residence," a frail woman's voice staggered. "But Tommy...I have—something came back to me. Something I sent to you." She sounded like a cartoon grandmother. Howard was astonished by her—he started to think it was an act by Dorothy, a gag she heard at the Avalon. "It said wrong address, but I can't get—I want to get the right address from you so I can send it back. The only thing I remember sending to you was your birthday card. So I guess that's what it is. But I need to get your right address. I don't want to send it back again. So call me and tell me what your right address is. I have PO Box 3052...El Sprentzo, California... um...9244. So please call and let me know what it really is. Thank you, hon. Bye."

The robot voice returned to announce, "End of message."

Howard stared at the phone as if another Martian flower had crawled out of the wallpaper. By now the smell of burning coffee paraded from the kitchen. He ran to the stove and dealt with that emergency. What was left of yesterday's tragic cup of coffee he poured down the sink. The faucet gasped when he forgot and tried to turn it on. He had to refill the pan with the water in a pickle jar and he set it aside to cook.

After all that commotion, Howard returned to the telephone. It didn't look Martian anymore. It was just a machine made of Bakelite, circuits and wires that would carry him in a current to a witch living in a water tower.

On the third ring, she answered, "Hello."

"Dorothy?"

"Yes. Hi Howard."

"Hi." All he said was her name and she knew it was him. "Are you done making feathers?"

She laughed. This wasn't Margaret Hamilton—she had a laugh you looked forward to. "Yes. You know what? You're the first one who isn't a witch to use a feather. Did you enjoy your flight?"

"Uhh…" he switched the phone to his other ear and admitted, "I don't think I'm ready to be a witch yet."

She laughed again. "It does take some practice."

"One thing though—you'll want to be careful, Dorothy. I ran into a kid hiding in the park who knows about you. I got his promise not to tell anyone, I made him an honorary detective and told him we were top-secret partners. But he did see you once before and told Samovar Betch."

He heard her sigh and say, "I'm not surprised. I've been careless. The big crow didn't help matters." He didn't like hearing her this way. "It's not easy being a witch. Maybe I should have let that big crow fly me away."

"No, you can't leave. We need you here. I've seen your magic firsthand, I know what you can do. Everyone else is stuck in a dream. Once the city wakes up, imagine what it will be like."

She was quiet. She might have been picturing that world.

Howard didn't know what else to say besides it would get better. We all have that power. He walked to the window and looked outside. "Hey—how about that? It stopped raining." It felt like magic. He wanted her to feel better and he cast the perfect spell. That's what he told her anyway.

He found his way to the stove again while she talked and checked the pan of water. It was nearly boiling. He never got to the end of a cup of coffee, but he kept trying.

"Witches don't tend to live very long," she told him matter-of-factly. "I just want to do good things before I'm gone."

"Miracles," Howard said, "that's what we need. That reminds me—" there was another reason he called. He told her about Sunny Jim and asked if her crystal ball could find that poor missing dog.

"Is this the sort of miracle witches will be called upon to do when the city wakes up?"

"It would mean the world to him."

"You're lucky I'm a good witch," she said.

"Are there bad ones?"

"Of course not," she quickly answered.

CHAPTER 13
The BAD WITCH

Edith Gale balanced the old dog over her broom. The few dead leaves on the tops of trees shook in her wake. She landed in the park in view of the water tower. A little earlier and she would have seen a crow big as a billboard. She made luggage handles on Oscar's back and lifted him onto the trail. While he stood there on the gravel, his rheumy eyes reflected the gray sky. A 112 year old man could relate.

Edith swiftly roped his leash to a tree stump and disappeared in a cloud of smoke. Oscar was the bait on the end of a hook. Wherever Edith Gale was, she was watching.

This was the image Dorothy found in her crystal ball—the water tower came into view, then turned into the gravel trail a hundred yards from her house, where a ghostly dog was tied to a tree stump on the familiar path. "I'm getting the name Oscar," she said. "That's him!"

She told Howard where Oscar was and they agreed to meet there as soon as Howard could put on dry clothes and get in the rocket car.

He left frogman footprints with his wet socks. He missed having a hot shower. What a luxury. Why did civilization keep falling apart? Water meters would go off and you were thrown back into the Medieval Ages.

As soon as he returned to the kitchen on the way to the door, wearing a charcoal coat and a black crumpled porkpie hat, the phone rang. He grabbed it. "Hello?"

It was Sunny Jim. "I just want to know if you got any leads."

"Actually, I do."

Sunny Jim begged, "What? Where's Oscar?"

"I'm on my way to get him now."

"Where's he at?"

Howard regretted telling, he winced and shut his eyes—that wasn't the way to handle a potential hostage situation. He hoped the rocket car would beat Sunny Jim to the park, he didn't want to put his new client in danger. But as it turned out, he put all four of them in danger.

Howard hung up and glanced at the cardboard car leaning by the radiator. As it dried, the corners warped. It was going to end up looking like a paper boat. Anyway, he didn't have time for that slow ride. The park was only seconds away by rocket car.

Before he got in behind the wheel, he looked out the garage window at the garden. There weren't any Martian flowers with a French reply. He let the curtain fall and went to his waiting car.

It growled down the muddy alley, steaming at the edge of Myrtle Street until he punched in the directions, then, with a snap and a howl, it shook Howard there.

He cut the motor. The windshield cleared and the water tower stilted ahead, across the parking lot, framed by trees.

The door made a lot of noise opening, as usual. He clambered to the pavement, crows were calling, a puddle revealed a blue bit of sky.

"Hello again," Dorothy said. She balanced on the curb, wearing silver shoes. She wore a green hood to protect herself from any wayward drops. He was close enough to read the same green color in her eyes.

"Hi Dorothy, thanks for your help."

"Thanks for making it sunny."

"What? I didn't—I can't really make the weather change." Except for his joke about the dogcatcher, Howard Plaid wasn't known for his sense of humor. Being a detective was a serious business...even if it meant selling umbrellas.

"Maybe you didn't know you could," she said with a smile. "Think what a great witch you would be."

"Yeah."

"You can allow a little rain now and then, but never so it's a surprise."

"Yeah...that would be quite a talent to have. I wish

I could help you with that, Dorothy. But I'm just a detective looking for a dog."

"Oh right," she remembered, hand to her lips like a Greek statue. "Oscar is ahead of us. We'll see him in a minute."

They left the parking lot for the gravel that took them into the bare trees. Howard watched them and said, "I looked at my garden before I left. I thought there might be a message for me."

"I don't think that will happen yet. Those flowers only grow when it's spring on Mars."

"When will that be?"

"Not for another year. Their seasons are different than here. It might even take a year for your Bonjour to reach her. Martian communication by flower takes its time."

A squirrel ran over a branch above them and they stopped to watch it go into its nest, a heap of leaves in the crook of a tree. Getting to Oscar didn't seem to be top priority. The gravel crunched like snow as they walked again. He listened and looked at her silver shoes. His were still muddy from the rain.

They both heard running behind them and they turned around together. Being a witch or being a detective made you wary.

"Howard!"

Howard Plaid rolled his eyes.

Sunny Jim ran at them like someone escaping a haunted house. He didn't seem acquainted with the fast pace; when he skidded to a stop he braced his hands on his knees.

"Hello, Sunny Jim."

Sunny Jim had to grab handfuls of air to say, "Where is he? Where's my dog?"

Dorothy told him, "We're almost there." She had seen Sunny Jim on the way. She had misjudged him though, she thought they'd find the dog long before him. She didn't know Sunny Jim put Oscar ahead of everything. "Hold on, we can walk together." They had to adjust their pace to Sunny Jim's shuffle, fast, but not fast enough to give him a heart attack. For a second Dorothy caught those eyes, wild and shiny as pennies left on a railroad track.

Howard informed Dorothy, "Sunny Jim and I used to be neighbors. He lived in the boarding house across the alley. Oscar was a puppy back then."

"My heart's racing," Sunny Jim puffed. He twitched and asked Howard, "You got a cigarette I can bum?"

That was just like Sunny Jim to take his last cigarette. After all they'd been through, Howard dug into his pocket and his fingers came out with tobacco and torn paper. Oh, the way the match flame caught that cigarette and turned it into smoke.

"There he is!" Sunny Jim cried out a cloud.

Dorothy tried to warn him, be careful, something isn't right, but it was no use, Sunny Jim saw his dog and skittered the gravel in his hurry. He noticed the other people on the path, but all he focused on was that old dog wobbling and lying down.

Howard was a few steps ahead of Dorothy and as he recognized the people around the dog, he held his arm out in front of her protectively.

"I knew it!" Samovar Betch rejoiced. "I knew you were in with the witches!" The Chief stood beside him with a revolver in his hand. Samovar swung his witch winch, a vicious hook tied to a loop of rope.

And that wasn't all—Otis Trillium waved across the path. He saw his daughter and held out his arms, "Dorothy!"

What a scene! Then, with an explosion of black smoke in the middle of the path, it got worse.

Edith Gale whirled out of nowhere and quickly shot a spell at Samovar Betch and another at the Chief. In their place on the ground, beside a coiled rope and below a police revolver falling in slow motion, were two frogs. Edith was spinning to fire again when Sunny Jim pulled the trigger in three successions.

Howard Plaid only thought to protect the witch behind him, shielding Dorothy with his charcoal suit.

One waterbullet hit Edith in the eye, instantly blinding the eye forever, as the Chief's gun struck the gravel path and went off. That bang and Edith's scream collided in the air. In the next second the Chief's gun was silent and black smoke churned Edith Gale from sight.

Sunny Jim threw himself onto his dog who hadn't responded to anything yet. Oscar's reflexes crept like sand in an hourglass, dragging him into the present.

"Howard!"

Dorothy didn't have the spell to turn back time. If only she did—what a difference a few seconds would make.

Howard fell. He could feel the blood seeping around his hand on his chest, but he felt no pain. The chickadees were singing. He could see the life leaving him, this bright world was dimming.

"Howard," Dorothy repeated, close to his ear. Her hand went over his, over his wound. She had tried to catch the bullet, but her hand was a little too slow and the slug slipped through her and stopped in him. "There's only way I can save you."

His eyes shut and opened. The Chief's bullet had done its job. He only saw her face and the circling kaleidoscope sky.

"Don't leave yet," she told him urgently, and with both her hands on him, she made a spell.

He was flying.

He was high over the land, floating on the wind.

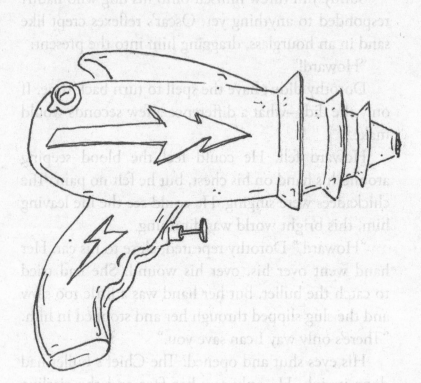

He saw the factory below, all the streets and familiar buildings, the sunshine sparkling on the bay, the little white and green ferry making a wake, and he then knew how a fish felt hooked to a line. He was pulled from the blue sky, right through a cloud. Seagulls reeled away from him crying, down, down, down. The park, the water tower, the tangled web of trees. He saw the gravel path, he saw Sunny Jim carrying Oscar away, he saw Dorothy holding the detective that was him, and he landed back where he had been. She lifted her hands and he could breathe.

"What was that?" He tried to sit up, but his head was spinning.

"Careful."

"What happened?"

She said, "You're alive again."

Howard remembered being shot, but when he held his hands off his coat, there was no blood. His fingers dug past the hole in his shirt, to his skin, smooth, unpunctured.

She said, "Bullets can't hurt you now. They pass right through...except for those waterbullets of course."

"I'm a witch?"

She nodded. "It was the only way I could save your life."

"You made me a witch?"

"If I didn't you would have died. I couldn't let that happen." She helped him get to his feet, put her arm around him while he wobbled.

"I don't know how to be a witch."

"Don't worry, Howard. We'll teach you."

"Can I do magic? Can I fly Sunny Jim and his dog back home?" He saw them stagger for the parking lot.

She smiled. "You have to start with little acts of magic like the girls in our schools."

He looked at the sun in the trees. It seemed so long since it glowed on everything. The birds had been hiding from the rain and now they were chattering happily. "Are we the only ones left?" Where he had last seen the Chief and Samovar Betch the ferns became home to two frogs. They would do alright living in there, no more offices, paperwork, axes or rocket cars. "Where did your father go?"

"He's gone now. We spoke while your spell took hold. He was anxious to get out of here—he was afraid Edith Gale would come back and turn him into a toad."

"Edith Gale?"

"She was the witch behind all of this. Are you ready for this, Howard? Edith Gale set this up. She caught Oscar, knowing Sunny Jim would tell you, knowing you would call me for help. Then she called Samovar Betch and told him I would be here.

Samovar telephoned my father who he was working for—sorry, I guess my dad wasn't getting results with you—and Samovar also told the police chief he would be exterminating a witch, to come along and see. Edith Gale used us all to get the Chief and Samovar so she could turn them into frogs and end the war. Of course, she didn't figure Sunny Jim would show up armed and ready for her. C'est la guerre."

"I thought you said witches couldn't hurt people?"

"That's not quite true. I just didn't want you to think that I could hurt you."

CHAPTER 14
A TELEGRAM

Howard Plaid was done being a detective. He was done storing water in his kitchen and sadly he was done ever trying to have a cup of coffee again. As a witch there wasn't much about his old life that he could carry with him. A couple suitcases would hold it all. He put them in the trunk of the rocket car.

Outside, the city was gray and silver again and it was raining around them but not on them. Howard was holding it back. He had that power after all. A big invisible umbrella branched over them and made a dry circle for them to walk on. Without even trying, Howard had done that. That magic came to him easily, as if it had been inside him all along like a dandelion bloom. Every witch had their own certain talent, he was lucky Dorothy brought that out in him.

The car trunk gave a clang as is shut. Soon they would be driving to the Trillium estate, the two-story house hidden in the woods was now theirs. That's what Otto Trillium was trying to tell his daughter. He was retiring, going to Mars where it was sunny and dry. Everything was hers. If she wanted the Water Department, it was hers too. He confessed witches had been working there for years. Clerks, accountants, drivers and crews, there were witches all throughout and nobody knew. Now was the start of whatever she wanted. Dorothy told Howard this was a new day—they weren't going to hole up in a garage or an empty water tower anymore. From now on, witches in Trillium would know where to go.

Howard was ready to leave Myrtle Street. It had been a bad day for the police—they lost their Chief, their best witchfinder, and the old Howard Plaid disappeared. All it took to end a war was for nobody to believe in it anymore.

Howard opened the squeaking door for Dorothy who was busy reading her crystal ball. As she got settled on the bench, she saw something and stopped him, "Oh! Before we go, you have to meet a turtle. It looks like it's in the garden."

"A turtle?" Then he recalled the one he found in a soup can. The one he set free in the pond.

"You go ahead," Dorothy said, "I'll wait here." She was fine, dry inside the car, holding that crystal ball full of sparkling light. It was waiting for him to move before it could turn into television again.

Howard waved and turned from the rusted fins and rocket nozzle, walking on a miraculous shadow around the corner of the garage. Dorothy wasn't watching him now, the crystal ball was showing her the future. Dots of rain had returned to the windshield outside. Whatever she was smiling at was blurred by the streaks on the glass.

Howard didn't notice anything unusual about the backyard garden. Winter made it mostly quiet. He walked to the aqueduct and stopped not too near it. A river trickled in it. He could feel the molten heat of it. In the middle of the garden, the pond bubbled with falling rain. Where was the turtle he was supposed to meet? A crow high in the chestnut tree watched him. Howard could have talked to it, but he didn't know that yet. He would have to wait for his first quarter at Trillium Witch Academy. By spring he would understand not just the animals but every bit of green transmission from the leaves. He would learn to recognize when a creature was calling him, and he wouldn't have to stand under an umbrella of his own making, searching the weeds for a turtle.

A gust ran across the garden and rattled leaves that weren't already tamped down by rain. The wind brought words too, everything in the world was alive in ways Howard Plaid had never thought about before. He heard the picket fence chatter, the birdhouse sneeze, and a rock at his feet gave a whistle. That got Howard's attention. He looked at the ground and this is what he saw:

The turtle pushed through the clover under the aqueduct arch. It paddled each leg with the slow determination of a windup toy. And like a dog with a newspaper in its mouth, it carried a note, rolled up tight as a cigarette. The turtle telegram ran out of steam when it hit Howard's shoe.

For someone used to writing on flowers and witchcraft magic, Howard didn't seem surprised. He only wondered if it would be a message from Mars, or from someone waiting for him in a rocket car.

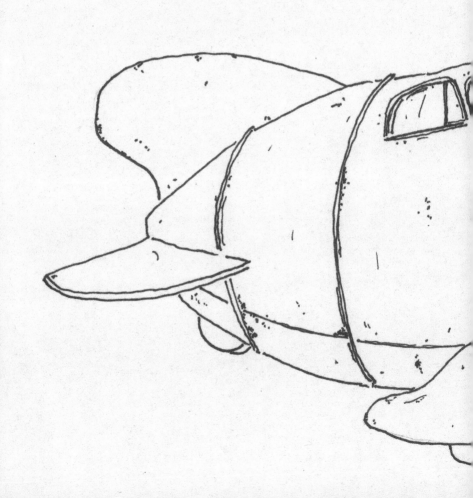

AFTERWORD

witches (and water

If you are a reporter for the *Herald*, and you have climbed 14 flights of stairs—sorry, the elevator is out of order again—to get to my rooftop apartment overlooking the city and you ask me that old chestnut, "Where did you get your ideas for *The Trillium Witch*?" here's what I'd tell you:

It began with the film noir idea in my notebook, about a detective and a witch.

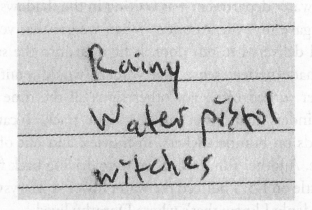

Now that I knew what the book was, I listened to its story unfold. Like music it was already there in the air, just waiting to become real. Once I was aware, I let it do the talking.

I heard about an island a long time ago, somewhere off our shore, owned by a millionaire. Like one of those 1930s Universal Pictures, it was stocked with wild animals from Africa. My friend used to steer his boat past there and catch glimpses of them in the trees. I couldn't resist giving the Trillium house a forest like that.

When I'm writing, everything around me becomes the landscape the book lives in: it builds itself with memories and messages, telephone calls, dreams, it all belongs. For instance, one night there was a loud knock on our door. The dogs barked. A woman from the water department was waiting in the shadows and she gave my wife a notice. When we got that yellow card delivered to our door, it fit right into the story. It made perfect sense that witches would want the water turned off. I got other signs all the time and reminders that I was on the right track. I caught words on bumperstickers, in movies, and out of the blue. Another time, when we were driving back from Seattle on I-5, I noticed the water tower in Marysville. Suddenly I knew that's where Dorothy lived.

I thought about witches (and water and the Land of Oz) and if rain can harm them I don't know how they could survive in the Pacific Northwest.

Then of course, our dog was a star of this book. She's on the cover, she's the inspiration for the showdown setting at the end of the book, in black and white film like *Somewhere in the Night.*

After that explanation, I would walk over to the window and look at the bay and the islands and the clouds that drift over everything. We can both hear it. *The Trillium Witch* is out there, floating like radio music. I just happened to tune into the signal, that's all.

The TRILLIUM WITCH

Writing & Drawings: Allen Frost

Written October 2020—January 2021

Illustration from *King Leopold's Slow Leak* (2000)

Books by Good Deed Rain

Saint Lemonade, Allen Frost, 2014. Two novels illustrated by the author in the manner of the old Big Little Books.

Playground, Allen Frost, 2014. Poems collected from seven years of chapbooks.

Roosevelt, Allen Frost, 2015. A Pacific Northwest novel set in July, 1942, when a boy and a girl search for a missing elephant. Illustrated throughout by Fred Sodt.

5 Novels, Allen Frost, 2015. Novels written over five years, featuring circus giants, clockwork animals, detectives and time travelers.

The Sylvan Moore Show, Allen Frost, 2015. A short story omnibus of 193 stories written over 30 years.

Town in a Cloud, Allen Frost, 2015. A three part book of poetry, written during the Bellingham rainy seasons of fall, winter, and spring.

A Flutter of Birds Passing Through Heaven: A Tribute to Robert Sund, 2016. Edited by Allen Frost and Paul Piper. The story of a legendary Ish River poet & artist.

At the Edge of America, Allen Frost, 2016. Two novels in one book blend time travel in a mythical poetic America.

Lake Erie Submarine, Allen Frost, 2016. A two week vacation in Ohio inspired these poems, illustrated by the author.

and Light, Paul Piper, 2016. Poetry written over three years. Illustrated with watercolors by Penny Piper.

The Book of Ticks, Allen Frost, 2017. A giant collection of 8 mysterious adventures featuring Phil Ticks. Illustrated throughout by Aaron Gunderson.

I Can Only Imagine, Allen Frost, 2017. Five adventures of love and heartbreak dreamed in an imaginary world. Cover & color illustrations by Annabelle Barrett.

The Orphanage of Abandoned Teenagers, Allen Frost, 2017. A fictional guide for teens and their parents. Illustrated by the author.

In the Valley of Mystic Light: An Oral History of the Skagit Valley Arts Scene, 2017. A comprehensive illustrated tribute. Edited by Claire Swedberg & Rita Hupy.

Different Planet, Allen Frost, 2017. Four science fiction adventures: reincarnation, robots, talking animals, outer space and clones. Cover & illustrations by Laura Vasyutynska.

Go with the Flow: A Tribute to Clyde Sanborn, 2018. Edited by Allen Frost. The life and art of a timeless river poet. In beautiful living color!

Homeless Sutra, Allen Frost, 2018. Four stories: Sylvan Moore, a flying monk, a water salesman, and a guardian rabbit.

The Lake Walker, Allen Frost 2018. A little novel set in black and white like one of those old European movies about death and life.

A Hundred Dreams Ago, Allen Frost, 2018. A winter book of poetry and prose. Illustrated by Aaron Gunderson.

Almost Animals, Allen Frost, 2018. A collection of linked stories, thinking about what makes us animals.

The Robotic Age, Allen Frost, 2018. A vaudeville magician and his faithful robot track down ghosts. Illustrated throughout by Aaron Gunderson.

Kennedy, Allen Frost, 2018. This sequel to Roosevelt is a coming-of-age fable set during two weeks in 1962 in a mythical Kennedyland. Illustrated throughout by Fred Sodt.

Fable, Allen Frost, 2018. There's something going on in this country and I can best relate it in fable: the parable of the rabbits, a bedtime story, and the diary of our trip to Ohio.

Elbows & Knees: Essays & Plays, Allen Frost, 2018. A thrilling collection of writing about some of my favorite subjects, from B-movies to Brautigan.

The Last Paper Stars, Allen Frost 2019. A trip back in time to the 20 year old mind of Frankenstein, and two other worlds of the future.

Walt Amherst is Awake, Allen Frost, 2019. The dreamlife of an office worker. Illustrated throughout by Aaron Gunderson.

When You Smile You Let in Light, Allen Frost, 2019. An atomic love story written by a 23 year old.

Pinocchio in America, Allen Frost, 2019. After 82 years buried underground, Pinocchio returns to life behind a car repair shop in America.

Taking Her Sides on Immortality, Robert Huff, 2019. The long awaited poetry collection from a local, nationally renowned master of words.

Florida, Allen Frost, 2019. Three days in Florida turned into a book of sunshine inspired stories.

Blue Anthem Wailing, Allen Frost, 2019. My first novel written in college is an apocalyptic, Old Testament race through American shadows while Amelia Earhart flies overhead.

The Welfare Office, Allen Frost, 2019. The animals go in and out of the office, leaving these stories as footprints.

Island Air, Allen Frost, 2019. A detective novel featuring haiku, a lost library book and streetsongs.

Imaginary Someone, Allen Frost, 2020. A fictional memoir featuring 45 years of inspirations and obstacles in the life of a writer.

Violet of the Silent Movies, Allen Frost, 2020. A collection of starry-eyed short story poems, illustrated by the author.

The Tin Can Telephone, Allen Frost, 2020. A childhood memory novel set in 1975 Seattle, illustrated by author like a coloring book.

Heaven Crayon, Allen Frost, 2020. How the author's first book Ohio Trio would look if printed as a Big Little Book. Illustrated by the author.

Old Salt, Allen Frost, 2020. Authors of a fake novel get chased by tigers. Illustrations by the author.

A Field of Cabbages, Allen Frost, 2020. The sequel to The Robotic Age finds our heroes in a race against time to save Sunny Jim's ghost. Illustrated by Aaron Gunderson.

River Road, Allen Frost, 2020. A paperboy delivers the news to a ghost town. Illustrated by the author.

The Puttering Marvel, Allen Frost, 2021. Eleven short stories with illustrations by the author.

Something Bright, Allen Frost, 2021. 106 short story poems walking with you from winter into spring. Illustrated by the author.

The Trillium Witch, Allen Frost, 2021. A detective novel about witches in the Pacific Northwest rain. Illustrated by the author.

CPSIA information can be obtained
at www.ICGtesting.com
Printed in the USA
LVHW031700140621
690189LV00018B/1217